A Cer

Monster

Prologue

Emerald County lies in Southwest Virginia, close to two hours outside of Richmond. Historically a quiet farm town and the home to many "mom and pop" shops and restaurants, Emerald claims just over 15,000 residents—a place where the beautiful countryside and old farmhouses draw in simpler people who live slower-paced lives. The school year is ruled by the various sports teams of Emerald County High, which draws in a significant chunk of the population for its football games in the fall, and although not as popular, still a fair turnout for the basketball and baseball teams in the spring. The summer is full of farmers doing their best to create a satisfying harvest in the fall and the local teenagers taking advantage of the hot summer air for bonfires and barn parties full of cheap beers and warm laughs as they reminisce about tall tales of themselves, one-upping each other from one fable to the next.

The front page of the local Emerald paper, "The Emerald Issues," is usually covered with an eye-catching crime of the century sounding phrase that led to an underwhelming low-level crime such as a daytime breaking and entering or perhaps a severe vehicle crash where someone lost control on a winding backcountry road. Although these events would never even see the light of day in a paper of a surrounding and more populated area, it was still considered significant news in Emerald. It would be the week's talk at the grocery store and the aforementioned sports games.

Lately, however, the papers have been plastered with horrific events that were the talk of this small town and the larger bordering counties. This small town's charm has been shaken by a series of murders, three, to be exact. Once the third murder was made public, true panic doused the county residents. "The Emerald Issues," which never seemed to top the sales of more than a few thousand copies a week, now saw sold-out paper kiosks within a few days of each publishing. Emerald did not have its own television news stations; rather, the residents tuned into the further Richmond channels, which had many segments to cram into their time slot. Although the killings had made a few television appearances, "The Emerald Issues" seemed filled with the latest and greatest, as the paper claimed.

The first murder was shocking enough. Emerald hadn't seen one in fifteen years before the first girl. The last murder to strike this quiet town was when the Sullivan boy went nuts and killed his parents in their sleep. Danny Sullivan was still referred to as the "Sullivan boy" when the murders were talked about, even though that "boy" was thirty-four years old. Sullivan was a known paranoid schizophrenic whose doctor suggested several times to his parents that he needed to be in a full-time facility for adequate care as the doctor believed his parents could not handle either the emotional stress or the physical time and care that went into it.

The schizophrenia set in during Danny's twenties, and it set in fast. His parents never could bring themselves to place him in a facility. They were heartbroken at his diagnosis but maintained that he was always such a sweet little boy and that he would never hurt anyone. It was the mind trap of the loving parents. Every time Danny had an increasingly violent outburst in the home or town, they still couldn't look past the beautiful memories they had of him when he was such a sweet and loving boy. Picturing him running to and kissing them, telling them he loved them, playing on the floor with his plastic Army men and trucks, and running in the backyard with the family dog. What parent would give up on their son who had always been so special to them? The love that they lived for ultimately took their lives.

One night, while Jack and Renee Sullivan slept, Danny crept into the bedroom and began stabbing his father in the stomach with a knife he had taken from the kitchen. Renee was awoken by his screams. Panic set in like a hot iron, and she bolted for the bedroom door, but Daniel was quicker. Renee was found stabbed to death in the entryway of the bedroom. Danny called the police immediately after and told the police what he had done. The reason? Demons were living inside their stomachs, staying alive by feeding off what Jack and Renee ate. Daniel killed his parents trying to save them.

The story of Danny Sullivan was still widely told in Emerald and, of course, became increasingly creepier and more sadistic as it was passed on from person to person. Danny now resided in a state hospital. To be released was not his fate, it seemed. Before the Sullivan murders, it had probably been close to twenty years earlier that the last murder had taken place. No one could barely remember the reason: two friends in business together that went sour and resulted in one shooting the other. A story that has been long forgotten in Emerald County.

When the first murder took place, the town was rattled. Debbie Robinson, nineteen years old, was found dead and naked in a ditch off Route 32, an abandoned industrial road. She was found raped, tortured, and murdered. The cause of death was determined to be multiple stab wounds to the abdomen. Debbie had just finished her first year at college and stayed home with her parents for the summer. The town wondered how such an unspeakable act could happen in a place like Emerald. Who was the killer? A resident? Was it someone passing through? Debbie had no natural enemies. She was a beautiful blonde girl, and although prettier than most girls she went to school with, she was still just as sweet as ever.

When first revealed, it was rumored to be an angry ex-boyfriend or perhaps a jealous boy who was in love with Debbie but did not receive the same affection. A handwritten note was left with the body that read, "She was most beautiful in the moonlight." The note made it more certain to police that Debbie's killer was in love with her. Debbie didn't date much, mostly preoccupying herself with school. Still, the police questioned a handful of young men that Debbie had dated and a few that wished they had, according to her friends. Young men from her hometown of Emerald and her University were investigated. Still, no solid leads indicated any of their involvement. However, without any doubts of the mind, it was certain to the citizens of Emerald that someone was extraordinarily bitter and sullen towards Debbie and that this person let loose an enraged outburst that could only be atoned for in hell.

Two weeks later, another girl was found. Twenty-two-year-old Hannah Vermond, a red-headed and pale-skinned waitress, was found floating naked in the Flat Rock reservoir. Another abominable scene. She was discovered by a group of teens looking forward to a night of light beer and cheap marijuana. Hannah, too, had been raped and murdered. Hannah's cause of death was determined to be strangulation. Like Debbie, Hannah was well-liked in town. Although a sarcastic attitude got the best of her at times, she was still the red-headed beauty queen of Emerald. "Emerald's Ariel" was her nickname throughout school. Another note was found with Hannah. Unlike Debbie's note that was found lying next to her body, this one was found on a folded piece of paper that had been force-fed into Hannah's mouth post-mortem. The note read, "Just in time for coffee." A note more perplexing than the first yet equally perverse in any context.

The police questioned if these notes were clues or just plain nonsense. They didn't seem to have any similarities in meaning other than that they were both handwritten and obviously from the same author. Once again, the town was in awe. Two unrelated murders would not happen in a place like Emerald. Considering the timeliness and similarity of the two, the possibility of them being related could not be ignored. The town began to discover that their assured thoughts of someone being ill-willed towards Debbie Robinson were now most likely erroneous. Suspicions arose in the town that it was the works of a madman, a serial killer in the making. The local police department was in disarray. With just fifty-three sworn police officers on the books, they lacked the resources larger departments took for granted. Only a few veteran detectives had experience working on cases such as these, which was the Sullivan case, but not much investigating was needed when you have a psychotic suspect willing to give a confession.

Emerald was governed by a small board of supervisors. Three individuals acted in lieu of a mayor that the bigger cities had. The two gentlemen and one lady that sat on the board were breathing down the neck of the Chief of Emerald Police, Colonel Anderson. Although usually supportive of the department, there was just over a year before the next election, and a quick solve of the case could abstain any lingering sour taste in the mouth of voters. The board feared that an ongoing and unsolved killing spree would ring in an entirely new board come election time.

One article from "The Emerald Issues" made claims of threats behind closed doors to hand the investigation over to the state police. The most senior member of the board, Charles Grimes, had concerns that the backwoods detectives may be too inept to handle such a case. Colonel Anderson combated these claims with assurance that his department was more than capable of handling the investigation and would not bow down to cheap threats from those without experience in dealing with police matters.

It was another month after Hannah that a third body was found. Jessica Shire, twenty-eight years old, was located in a cornfield on the Henderson Farm, hanging naked from an old scarecrow post. She was not hanging by a noose around her neck but by her hands, which had been stretched out to her sides and nailed to the post. The cause of death was later determined to be asphyxiation.

Another young blonde female, yet not as well-liked as the others. Jessica was beautiful, and she knew it. She used her beauty to get what she wanted and twisted the hearts and souls of men who dared to get involved with her. Her mother used to say, "She taught the class in sass," due to her apathetic attitude towards others. Around Jessica's neck hung a paper sign that was held together with frayed brown twine. The sign read, "If a swan must fly, she must first spread her wings." The script left an eerie aura over the body. With her arms spread like that on the post, one might compare it to a sadistic rendering of the crucifixion of Jesus. The hands were nailed just the same. However, her feet were not crossed and nailed as the Christians' savior's feet were. Here, they simply hung straight down. It was indeed a horrific sight to see. Although Jessica was a cruel girl at times, a grim and abhorrent death such as this was not deserved by anyone.

Jessica's death was the nail in the coffin for Emerald Police. There was officially a serial killer among them. Both the residents and the board of Emerald were demanding answers. The stories were becoming regular airings on television stations around central Virginia and spreading elsewhere. Colonel Anderson knew there would be a tightening noose around his neck if questions were not answered promptly. Orders were rapidly passed down the chain of command for case assignment.

Chapter 1

There was heat. Not the warmth of a glistening sun on a summer day, or even that felt in the Sahara Desert, but true heat. It was a heat that had never been felt before. A heat so intense that the sweat seemed to evaporate mere seconds after leaving the skin's pores. *'Who else has felt this before?'* This heat, which seems almost uninhabitable, yet surrounds a man living and breathing in its grasp.

Edward Jackson awoke on a stone-covered floor. He could feel the rough, hard surface beneath him but had not been awake long enough to gather his surroundings. As his eyes began to adjust, he could see there were almost no surroundings to observe. *'Where am I?'* he thought to himself. *'Am I Blind? No.... there.'* His mind had deceived him, and there was soon sight.

The darkness fenced him in, but with a faint ambient light that loomed over him. Edward was lying face down on the stone and began to push himself up with his weak arms. There was an intense fatigue in his muscles that he could only imagine one would feel on their deathbed. His arms continued to quiver as he worked to lift his upper body from the ground. He looked down at the yellowish stone beneath his body and felt the dry, dusty sand on his palms and knees as he struggled with his posture.

His eyesight was beginning to adapt better to his environment. The stone was yellow and old, appearing to have been laid thousands of years before, but still not in a dilapidated state. It resembled that of the great Mayan and Roman ruins- ancient yet still intact. The ominous light surrounding him had a dull cherry hue, but no light source seemed present.

Edward was then able to bring himself up enough to lift his waist off the ground and roll over to sit up on his bottom. It was at this point he noticed he was naked. He looked down in confusion as his buttocks scraped the gritty floor. He felt a rush of panic as he hastily covered himself with one of his hands. Edward's eyes conformed a bit further in the darkness and began to look around him. The heat was still unbearable, yet there seemed no place to seek refuge from it. He could see the heat rising off the stone beneath him, although the air seemed to hold the same dense torridness. Edward felt a thirst that needed to be quenched, but no water was present.

With his mind more focused, he could now identify a possible direction of the light source. In the distant darkness, a horizon seemed to unfold before him. Edward was unsure if the horizon truly existed and contemplated it being a mirage caused by extreme heat and fatigue, like a stranded man in the desert dying of dehydration that wanders towards a river or pond that exists only in his mind.

Although the light remained a murky presence, the newfound horizon offered a birthplace for its existence. Edward stared frozen at it with uncertainty. A heavy blanket of fear smothered him at this moment, and although the terror grew at the thought of going closer to the light, it seemed his only course for refuge. He knew he couldn't linger in the darkness forever, or he would succumb to the heat; it was time for him to move.

Despite the unforgiving heat that encompassed him, Edward seemed to remain in a frozen state. He changed positions from sitting on his butt to getting into a crawling stance on his hands and knees. He moved his left hand that was shielding his genitals from view, though there was no one around to see. *'Too damn dark to see in here anyhow.'* He thought to himself.

As he forced his limbs to carry him, his muscles felt the burden of an ant carrying an elephant. It wasn't long before he reverted to a prone state and began to pull himself with his dead arms. The loose sand on the stone began imprinting on his skin as he slid across it. The tiny tears in his flesh stung like a wasp as the salt from the stone seeped into them. He gritted his teeth together to help combat the pain, but it brought little relief to him. Edward figured the stone may be hot enough to cauterize any real damage.

As Edward crawled towards the horizon, it felt as if he was not alone. He could often hear both quick and light footsteps and slow and heavy trotting ones around him. A few times, the air above him seemed to move with a swish, as if something had flown over his head. *'Are there animals in here? Bats?'* he wondered. Edward was confident he was being tracked by something or someone.

When he stopped and turned his head in the darkness, the movement around him ceased, yet it was replaced with what seemed like laughter. The laughs resonated from what could have been miles away. Yet, the absence of surroundings allowed the sound to carry an incredible distance. *'Where the fuck am I? Is this all a nightmare?'* Indeed, he would be awake soon. As Edward focused on the laughs, he also began to detect the sounds of something else looming in the gaps between the bellowing; those sounds were screams.

Edward began to crawl faster to the light. As fear crept up quickly in his soul, he forced his arms to drag him faster. The sand and debris on the stone continued to scratch and score his hot skin as he moved. Were the screams getting closer or further away from him as he moved? He could discern such a thing if he took a moment to halt, but such a hiatus may allow whatever was making those footsteps to catch up to him. That was simply not an option.

As he approached the light, it seemed to grow, yet so did the heat. A foul stench began to arise in his nostrils, but he could not identify it. Up ahead, the horizon finally seemed to have an end. The stone now appeared to have a sudden drop-off, a cliff of sorts. Edward gritted his teeth again as his arms forced the last few grudging pulls and grabbed the edge of the stone cliff with his raw and chaffed fingers. Edward looked over the ledge expecting to find an abyss, yet what scarred his eyes was quite a hideous sight.

There was a lake of fire beneath him, and within the lake flailed the bodies of hundreds. The cliff encircled the lake, creating a pit. He identified the source of the screams and the smell everywhere he looked. The stench of burning flesh continued to offend his sense of smell with great strength. The people in the lake were very much alive and eminently aware of what was happening to them. The screams were like nothing he had heard. They were the screams of pure anguish and suffering. These screams pleaded for the suffering to end, but that end would not come. Their skin seemed to burn and melt off their bodies as they convulsed in unbearable anguish.

Among the people were other creatures that stood before them. These creatures were the source of the hideous laughs; creatures he could only imagine were demons. *'Am I in hell?'* Edward wondered. As his eyes wandered the pit, he realized that humans and other foreign creatures were also around the lake. On the far side, he witnessed a lizard-like creature raping a young woman. Although the woman screamed, her face remained in a dazed stare, making it hard to determine if the screams were from the pain of this massive creature forcing himself inside of her or just from the sheer terror that surrounded them. Her body was alive, but her eyes were quite dead. Her soul had dissolved its existence long ago.

There was a man just a few dozen feet from the woman. He was being eaten alive by another creature. This creature was not lizard-like but resembled some sort of bovine animal with hooves and human-like hands. The man screamed and clawed at the beast as it feasted on his stomach, yet the beast did not seem to notice.

Other strange creatures soared above the fire, screeching an awful cry and hissing at what lay below in the lake as they flapped their scaly wings. Razor-sharp talons hung below them, and their eyes were an intense red that outshined the fire beneath. As Edward's eyes swallowed the visions around him, there was not a death in his sight. This was an eternal punishment that death would be a relief from. These people were not allowed death.

In the center of all the madness sat another creature. This creature was not laughing with the others yet sat on a throne with a smirk of pleasure. It appeared to have short red hair about its body with massive black horns that protruded from its head. His eyes were also black, yet somehow seemed to glow as he looked down at the horror beneath him. This place could have only been the birthplace of Satan and yet the final resting place for all evil. As Edward marveled at this being, the creature's attention was suddenly taken by something. The beast lifted his chin away from his chest and faced above. Edward could see his massive nostrils flaring from his position. The creature could smell something...new, and Edward knew it was him. The creature's head suddenly shot left of Edward's position, causing him to freeze in fear. His petrified body witnessed the creature lift his left arm towards him and point with his long hair-covered finger. The beast shouted something that Edward could not identify as it was not in English but in some sinister-sounding tongue.

At that moment, Edward suddenly felt the ground beneath him begin to shake as he heard the heavy footsteps from earlier return behind him; however, there was an urgency about them this time. He was suddenly lifted into the air before Edward could turn around to see what was approaching him. As his body departed the floor, he was swung around by his arms, feeling as though they were pulling from the socket until he was facing the opposite direction.

Edward could now see that a great beast was holding him, shaking him effortlessly. The beast's hands had the strength of a bear, yet also could squeeze his limp arms in its grasp. The beast was a dark swine creature with even darker pits where the eyes should be. The swine gaped open its large mouth and spoke with a deep, robust voice that resonated as if a chorus of a thousand voices powered it. It shouted in Edwards's face, spewing a putrid breath into his lungs, "What kind of God would allow a hell like this!" The beast then launched Edward from his grip into the pit. As he flew, he stared at the beast above him. His soul seemed to leave his body as he crashed into the lake below...

Chapter 2

Edward Jackson awoke in a heavy pant. He was drenched in sweat, and his lungs wheezed, gasping for fresh air as he lunged out of his nightmare. Edward often suffered nightmares when he slept, which seemed like nature's cruel joke since he hardly ever slept. Officially diagnosed with insomnia three years prior and a nightmare disorder two years before that. Although having a nightmare disorder is not as severe as night terrors, it still took a physical toll on him, almost creating a phobia of sleep. Edward referred to it as his circle of fuckery. Can't fall asleep most nights, and when he does? Nightmare on fucking Elm Street. *'You win God.'*

Edward had suffered from frequent nightmares since he was a teenager. His father left when he was still young and vibrant, leaving Edward's mother alone to raise him and his younger sister, Elaine. At fifteen, the nightmare that started them all happened. A noise was heard on the night of the Jackson home. Edward and Elaine had heard their mother scream, followed by thumps and shuffles. Edward slept just across the hall from her room upstairs. He was the first in and discovered the nightmare. His mother, Moreen, had been stabbed to death. Edward saw the blood-covered bed, sheets, and floor. His mother propped up against the nightstand, letting her last breath escape, and she looked into Edward's eyes. "I love you." The last words she seemed to muster without any air left in her. Edward saw the knife on the floor next to her and picked it up. He stood there in disbelief at what had happened.

At that time, Elaine had worked up the courage to investigate herself. She entered to see Edward standing over their mother, sobbing with the knife still in his hand. The police later determined this had been the work of an outside intruder. The doors to the home were found to still be locked. Edward and Elaine professed to the police they never heard anyone come in or flee. Edward argued he would have met him at the landing above the stairwell on his way to his mother. The police shrugged this off, discrediting it up to traumatized kids. A closed but unlocked window was found in the kitchen. This was labeled as the entry and exit point of the intruder in the official report. No one was ever charged, not even a potential suspect.

Edward and Elaine were sent to live with an aunt and uncle for the remainder of their adolescent years. Once adults, Edward and his sister grew distant and barely spoke to each other to this day. Edward had been in and out of therapy his whole life since. Elaine had as well, along with a script for every bottle of pills she could to help cloud her mind. During the roughest of times, bottles of drugs were obtained by other means with no prescriptions issued. The death seemed to follow and haunt them both through the years, never appearing to let up its deadly grasp.

A pastor at the funeral stated, "There is truly never enough time to fully grieve the loved ones we've lost; it simply just gets easier in time." Those words have always stuck with Edward. They were the most genuine words he had ever heard. It had gotten more manageable in time, but the pain would never fully dissipate, and he would never fully heal.

The black digital clock that Edward had owned since high school showed 7:00 p.m. in dull green numbers. It was a cool night for mid-September in Virginia. Edward enjoyed the crisp breeze coming in through the open window on his hot, sweaty body. He could smell the season change in the air. Autumn was here. As he rolled on his side, his back shot from hot to cold as the cool breeze reacted with the sweat on the back of his old black T-shirt. It ignited a shiver that Edward quickly shook off. Although the evening was in, the sun was still prevalent, hanging high in the sky and creating an orange overtone. This was Edward's favorite time of the year.

Edward sat up and swung his legs off the side of the bed. His sweaty feet, finally able to breathe, began to cool off on the cold hardwood plank floor. Nearly gouging his eyes right out of his head, Edward pulled out the crust deep in the corners of his eyeballs with the tips of his fingers. He went to the bathroom and let loose his extremely backed-up bladder. As Edward relieved himself, his eyes wandered around the bathroom. It was indeed overdue for a cleaning, but he knew he would be in no rush to tackle this job. He was not one for house guests. To think of it, Edward was confident he had never had a guest in his house before. This tiny farmhouse-style home he had bought years ago had only seen Edward's face since its purchase. A lonely yet content home it was for him. Edward flushed, skipped the wash, and walked to the kitchen to make something to eat.

It wasn't unusual for Edward to sleep late into the day like this. Most days, he gave up trying to sleep at night, knowing it would never come. If he attempted, he usually watched old cartoons such as The Simpsons or King of the Hill. The light chuckles it gave him seemed to ease his troubled mind, yet he would still find himself awake until dawn. It was easier for him to lie down in the early afternoon to get any real rest.

Edward opened the fridge and pulled out a carton of eggs. He stood over the stove, still wearing nothing more than his flannel pajama pants and an old t-shirt as his eggs cooked. He added his usual ingredients and then scraped them into a bowl. He then retreated to the couch in the living room and turned on the television just in time to catch the evening news.

Emerald did not have its own stations and most of what the local cable providers put on were out of Richmond. It started with the live coverage of a near-fatal crash on Interstate 95 just outside of the city. A coupe-style sports car blew a tire out, causing the driver to lose control, and swung right under the rear end of a tractor-trailer. Even though the rear of the trailer rolled right over the sports car, somehow, the driver survived. He had been med-flighted to a local trauma center and was currently in surgery. Still, the reporter advised viewers that he was "expected to pull through." Edward knew none of the viewers cared about the outcome of these things, just another mindless attention grabber for views.

Once sports and weather were out of the way, the real excitement came. Right before his eyes was a recap of his latest work, Jessica Shire. Edward immediately stopped chewing his eggs and sat there momentarily with the remnants still in his mouth before finally swallowing. He slowly placed his bowl down on the wooden coffee table in front of him and sat back as the news anchor gave his speech, police photos being displayed on the screen behind him.

The young black anchorman spoke in the usual "anchorman" tone. "The residents in Emerald County are still in fear as a sequence killer is still on the loose." *'Sequence killer?'* Edward thought to himself. He didn't like that term. *'Who uses the term sequence killer? Perhaps serial killer was too cliché for this young aspiring anchor.'* Edward didn't think of himself as a serial killer. That's what the uptight television people called him, but they didn't understand. Serial killer sounded a bit too TV for Edward. That term was too famous for a nobody like him.

The anchor continued. "Local County Police Chief John Anderson states that his officers are still on the hunt for the person responsible, who he says is a highly disturbed individual." *'What the fuck, seriously? Disturbed?' What a fucking asshole.'*

The young anchor continued to ramble on as they played old footage of the crime scenes showing where the bodies were discovered. Yet, any footage or photos showing the bodies were distorted with a blurry blob. Edward didn't need them to show what was behind the blurriness. That was still fresh in his mind, like a new canvas art piece where you could smell the new paint.

As the news continued to cover the story, Edward could feel the blood flow steadily increase to his penis. For Edward, it was hard to see the clips and not replay the highlights in his head. It was only seconds before he had a full erection in his pants. He began to slowly rub at it with his hand over the top of the fabric. After a minute, he slipped his hand down under his underwear and began to stroke himself. He closed his eyes and rotated images of the different girls in his mind. He could almost feel their skin against his. He could practically grasp their smell as he imagined himself pressing his nose against the back of their skull as he fucked them from behind, just as he had. He could feel their hair on his face. He gripped himself harder the faster he stroked until he felt himself about to cum. He suddenly stopped himself. His breathing was still fast and hard. Such an arousal was not to be wasted in a towel or an old sock.

Nothing could replace the feeling of soft, warm flesh. It wasn't about sex. It wasn't about getting off. For Edward, it was the skin-to-skin contact with a woman. The sex was great, but nothing compared to the intimacy he felt with his body against another. Edward thought only a fool could claim this was the doing of a sex-craved man. It was so much more than that.

It had been three weeks since he had felt Jessica's skin and smelled that beautiful blonde hair. It was time for him to feel the touch he craved again, the connection he needed. It was a need, after all.

The anchor finished his story; "Police are still without suspects at this time and are urging anyone with information to please come forward." Edward looked out the window to his left. The sun was beginning to fade below the tree line and would soon be dark. Edward took a long, deep breath through his nose and smelled the air turning from summer to fall as he watched the ball of fire in the sky drift through the sway of the trees. Edward was off work today and tomorrow and wanted to enjoy his free time. It was a new night, and it was time to hunt.

Chapter 3

Emerald County, Thursday, September 15th at 7:30 p.m. Detectives Michael Bradley and Daniel Lugo sat at their desks as the evening news had just finished on the old and out-of-date box television mounted in the corner of the room. Both detectives had just spent the last ten minutes with massive pits in their stomachs as they watched their case displayed on the news to God knows how many people. Nothing seemed worse than watching a bunch of pompous-ass reporters who had probably never even stepped foot in Emerald talk about their town and the horrors that were happening.

Detective Bradley ranted, "Why is it that every goddamn time they air that story, they have to emphasize that we don't have any suspects?" Detective Lugo didn't respond at first. He looked out of the corner of his eyes and gave it some rational thought before giving any input. "I like it." He responded. Michael shot his head over in a snap, "Why?"

With his arms crossed over his chest, Daniel slightly shrugged his shoulders. "This guy is on top of the world right now. You know the asshole is watching the news every night, hoping this shit gets played. These guys feed off it. Every time he hears the news say we don't have any suspects, he is more confident that he won't get caught. With confidence comes complacency. And when complacency hits, that's when he'll slip up and when we will get him." Michael shook his head as he began to speak; "We don't even know if this guy is a guy..." Daniel slipped in with a rebuttal. "Most serial killers are white males."

"So what?" Michael shot back and continued, "We don't have anything on this...person. You talk about waiting for complacency to kick in, great. We already have three dead women...how many more will die before his first slip-up?" Daniel once again didn't say anything right away.

Michael and Daniel had been partners for years. There were only six detectives in a department of just over fifty officers. Generally, the detectives worked their cases solo and would only recruit the help of others for cases they needed help on, such as a string of robberies or a rape; however, due to the rarity of murders in Emerald, it was immediately decided by a higher pay grade that the department's two best detectives would work it together. There were a few detectives with more experience and tenure with the department. Still, it was well known that tenure doesn't always equate to capability and a good work ethic. Detectives Bradley and Lugo were still young and quite ambitious. They worked well together and had been friends since the day they met.

Michael Bradley was an impressive officer. He was a handsome white male who everyone liked. Even the subjects he questioned always seemed to like him, which is probably why so many confessed to him in the interrogation room. He was extraordinarily gung-ho and loved nothing more than catching suspects. Some wondered if he genuinely cared that much about his cases or if solving them just stroked his ego. Either way, the supervisors didn't seem to care. The department and the public wanted results and cases finished promptly, and Detective Bradley did that.

Daniel Lugo was the more reserved of the two. A Puerto Rican male who was very logical in his thinking, he seldom asked a suspect a question he didn't already know the answer to. He often states, "I always ask the questions I already know the answer to first, to gauge if the person is a liar; that way, I know if I can trust the answers given to me for the questions I don't know." Lugo often came off as more apathetic than he intended to be. It was not an issue of caring; he undoubtedly was. Lugo just lacked the ability to display emotions that others exuded so effortlessly. Although the more intelligent of the two, he lacked people skills. This is where he bonded and worked well with Bradley, who, although he was also brilliant, could get anyone to talk.

Daniel finally chimed back in, "I still think it's a male; women aren't sick enough in the mind to do that shit. And all three women show signs of rape...how's that for a woman suspect?" Michael smiled mildly at Daniel's matter-of-fact tone. "No semen found on any of the girls, object penetration?" Daniel shook his head. "Dude was just wearing a condom; why are you so stuck on the possibility of it being a female killer anyways?" Michael let out an annoyed sigh and leaned back excessively in his chair. He looked at the case board filled with pictures and dry-erase marker scribbles for possible motives and theories. He pondered his thoughts for a moment, then looked back at Daniel. "Look, I think it's a male too. In fact, I feel it in my gut just like you, but until we can prove it's a male, I don't want to rule out anything."

"I agree..." Daniel immediately replied, "But we still need to lead with the most likely. Besides, all the messages were handwritten, and the penmanship was sloppy at best. That ain't no girl's writing."

Michael got up, walked to the board, and uncapped a green dry-erase marker, half sure it was in its last few days of life. Both detectives had spent the last few months writing lists of motives, suspect possibilities, clue meanings, and some diagrams. Somehow, this little marker survived through it all, even if just barely.

"Well, let's start at the top again for round three hundred and sixty-two…. what all do we have?" Daniel immediately started gathering everything in his mind. He didn't need to look at the files with all the evidence because he had already read them a thousand times and memorized them. "Well, the obvious…no suspect description. No gender, age, or race. No known vehicles either, for that matter. All three girls were alone at the time they were abducted and killed. Hell…they were all found before there was enough time for anyone to report them missing." Michael stepped in, "Yeah, but two of the girls lived alone. It usually takes missing work or a family function before anyone notices they're gone."

"What about girl one, Debbie?" Daniel asked. "She was home visiting from college… just about to head back, but she was staying with her parents. Why didn't they report her missing?" Michael replied, "Well, she was taken after visiting with old friends on her way home. Parents assumed she just got drunk and was crashing with a friend for the night. But none of these reasons matter anyway. Trying to figure out why none of the girls were reported missing doesn't help us figure out who did it."

"I like to have an answer for everything," Daniel replied.

"What else do we have?" Michael pondered the board again for something else. "All the girls were wet when we found them, or at least their hair was wet."

"Girl two, Hannah, was found in the reservoir; that's a given," Daniel answered. Michael pursed his lips and rolled his head over at Daniel, "Stop doing that girl one, girl two shit. They have names." Daniel rolled his eyes and ignored his comment. "Do you think he bathed them?" With his lips still pursed together, Michael began to rock his head from side to side as he contemplated this idea and let out an exhausted sigh. "Perhaps. That would explain why no DNA was recovered from any of the scenes, or at least for the first two girls, and that's what I'm predicting from the lab since I haven't heard anything."

Still ignoring Michael's comment, Daniel added, "Girl three...everything for her is still being processed at the state lab. It could be several more weeks or so before we know for sure nothing was recovered. I'm hopeful they will find something." Michael let out a big sigh while still staring at the board. "Doubt it. It's been almost two months since Debbie, or girl one as you put it, and we have nothing to show for it." In an almost ashamed tone, Daniel replied, "I know. What about those crazy messages on the bodies? Still no idea what they could mean? I'm not sure if the guy is leaving us clues because he wants to get caught or he is just an arrogant asshole fucking with us by leaving nonsense that means nothing."

"It means something." Michael replied with an astounding assurance in his voice and continued, "I know it does, but finding out what it means could be as tolling as finding out who this fucker is. But he wants to be caught, or at least the girls to be found." Detective Lugo concurred, "Yeah, the notes for one. And none of the bodies were hidden. Debbie was left off an abandoned road but still traveled by high school kids often to go off-roading in the fields. Hannah left at Flat Rock, and Jessica nailed to a damn cross. He had to know they would all be found within a day or two." Michael, thinking out loud, mumbled, "He's from here...He lives here."

Daniel got up from his chair and stretched out his sore back. "Look, we've been at this non-stop for weeks, and my wife is gonna be pissed if I come home at midnight again. Let's call it a night, and we'll call the state lab first thing in the morning and tell them we need official results for girls one and two and see if anything is promising for girl three now or we're coming up there and not leaving until we do." Michael slightly hung his head and nodded gently. "Alrighty, I agree. Let's take the night to relax and forget about all this shit. We can come at it again tomorrow with fresher minds. Go ahead; I'll be right behind you. Have a good night, man." "You too, brother," Daniel said back.

Michael watched him gather his belongings and head for the door. Just before he exited, Michael shouted to him, "Just remember, we're working on the crime of the century here...by the time this is over, we'll be known everywhere as the detectives that solved it all or fucked it all up." Daniel stood with the door ajar, momentarily pondering Michael's comment, and then simply replied, "Crimes." He turned and headed out the door.

Michael then wandered over to the window and gazed over the now-darkening town around him as he watched the town folk walk about the sidewalk. After a minute, he spotted Daniel walking to his car and leaving. Michael continued to watch until his car was out of sight. He looked back up to the sky, took an extended breath, and sighed heavily, causing the glass to form a foggy cloud. He watched the fog quickly dissipate before him, revealing his reflection again in the glass. Michael, too, grabbed his things and headed home.

Chapter 4

Edward clunked down the wooden stairs on his porch in his old black leather boots. They were his favorite, and he had worn them for years. The leather was beginning to cross the line from broken in to broken down, but Edward didn't care. The air outside was crisp and clean. It was starting to cool for the night, and an invigorating presence entered his mind when he inhaled deeply, smelling the crisp autumn leaves that were beginning to fall. Just a few more weeks before he could smell the sweet frost of winter in the air.

It was just a short walk to where his truck was parked. As his feet shuffled across the bricks, he could feel the crunch and crumble of small twigs that had fallen with the leaves. His boot also caught a few rocks that had tumbled onto the path. Edward was sure there were more rocks in the grass and walkway than in the driveway. But getting the drive re-graveled was the lowest rung on his ladder of worries.

Edward climbed into his old Ford pick-up truck parked next to his pole barn and pressed in the clutch to start it. The engine took a second to turn but then boasted a deep roar once it fired up. Edward placed the truck in reverse, let his foot off the clutch, and felt the truck roll back slowly onto the grass. The sun had illuminated the pasture adjacent to his property.

The house behind his could barely be seen by the naked eye. Edward sometimes used an old pair of binoculars to take a gander now and then. The cows, however, came right up to the property line. The sun silhouetted their shadows across the tall grass that always seemed to sway regardless of the wind. He sat for a second to take in nature's painting and then placed the truck into first gear and took off. As he left the property, he took one last peek over his left shoulder at the fields, picking up a pair of calves that seemed to be chasing each other. He focused back on the road and gave a half-hearted wave to a passing vehicle. Everyone out here seemed to wave, whether they knew you or not. That was just life in the country.

It was only fifteen minutes into town. Traffic was light, as it usually is in this town. Emerald is mainly a farming town; most people head in early for the work that looms over them. One of the local taverns, Benny's, was still open with around twenty customers inside. It is not unusual in Emerald for the bars to have a fair amount of business on any given night. This town really likes its alcohol.

Edward always assumed that half the whiskey the Emerald joints sold was probably supplied by one of the few illegal distilleries in town. There were plenty of people here who had tried their hand at distilling. Most probably weren't good at it, although they would never admit it. Edward always assumed they figured it made them more "country" or perhaps just trying to live out like the legends the generations before them claimed to be. Edward parked his truck in the lot and walked across the dusty, disintegrating asphalt lot to head inside.

An immediate aroma of the sawdust that covered the wood plank floor coated Edward's nostrils. Whiskey and beer were in a battle for second place. Edward walked to the bar and ordered a stout. He sat for a moment, drinking his brew, glancing at the crowd. He let the first few sips saturate his taste buds, almost giving it a swish before swallowing. The beer left a dark, malty taste in his mouth.

It was an older gathering tonight, more aged than usual. Edward was only thirty and felt he might be the youngest in the room. He then spotted a group of college-aged kids who all seemed to be leaving the restrooms together. Two males and three females. They returned to an empty beer mug-covered table just beyond the other side of the bar. Edward thought to himself that the males were fuckboys and obviously overcompensating with attire and poor jokes. Those girls wouldn't be out of sight of them anytime soon. The looks on the girls' faces went from content to indifferent as their childish competition for 'who can be the biggest douche bag' continued. The girls were unlucky for being in their company, but at least not in the company of Edward unlucky.

Edward then set his sights on a beautiful woman by herself just a few tables away from the bar against the side wall of the tavern. She appeared to be about a decade older than himself. She seemed to be enjoying a nice glass of whiskey and was focusing her attention on the television, which was showing prime-time football. Dallas was trailing Green Bay, his favorite team, but he had no interest in the game right now.

The woman was petite and had long dark hair. Her skin was tan but appeared to be natural, not torched to death in a bed. She was beautiful for being alone, yet here she was. Perhaps a divorcee or possibly a widow. Either way, the lady looked to be out of her element here. Not quite nervous, not entirely confident. She appeared to want company but would not dare invite herself. She had surely been out of the dating life for a while and, perchance, waiting for someone to take a leap. *'Is she waiting for me?'* Edward's left eyebrow seemed to raise itself at this thought. Quite intrigued, Edward decided to give her a chance.

As he walked over, the woman quickly noticed his approach and blushed. She has most likely been approached by men often in settings such as this. She could identify it immediately, although it probably was rare for someone of Edward's age to make the approach. Her age seemed to grow with every step he took, less hidden by the cheap lights that dangled above them. Edward still found her intriguing; she would still suit him just fine. The woman was quite attractive for her age, which gave her an intimidating aura. A young man would surmise that a woman that good-looking at that age could only be tamed by a man, not a boy. Edward was going to be that man. He walked up until he was standing just two feet away from the table and made eye contact with the woman. Their eyes lingered with each other for just a few seconds, exposing her deep brown eyes. "Hey there, can I buy you a drink?" Edward asked softly but confidently. The brunette blushed harder, looked down at her drink, and began stirring the contents inside by whirling the glass in small, elegant circles. "Umm... I'm not sure if that's a real good idea." She let out a small giggle as she replied, this time looking up for what felt like an eternity, waiting for an answer. Her eyes were quite beautiful; their boldness seemed to lock Edward's own into hers.

"Why not? It's just a drink...and if you don't want to talk to me afterward, you only lose a few minutes of your life to some lousy conversation and still get a free drink out of it." Edward was unsure if her remark was a ploy for him to try harder or hope he wouldn't try. '*Well shit, I came this far.*' Edward pulled out a chair and sat across from her as if inviting himself. "Okay." the woman chuckled. She smirked at Edward as he sat down, seemingly impressed by his offer.

And like he said, in the worst-case scenario, she would score a free drink.

"Okay?" There was surprise in Edward's voice. As the words escaped his lips, even he was confounded, as if he were surprised, she said yes. Edward had become good at playing this game, almost assured of what women were prone to accepting his solicitation and who would most certainly give a firm no. Yet this lady had given him doubts of either turnout. She was, however, tonight's golden ticket.

Shannon felt reluctant about the situation but was not turned off. In her heart, she knew she had come here not hoping for attention but also not avoiding it. Shannon, who had just ended a several-year-long relationship with another man, had felt damaged and unwanted. Getting hit on by older, younger, single, and even married men helped her shed the skin of insults she had endured and let herself become in her mind. Whether she decided to act on anything with those men or not, a compliment was a compliment.

She had worked the courage to leave and not look back. In her mind, she could surely muster a conversation with a handsome stranger if she had tolerated that asshole. "Yeah, sure, you seem innocent enough."

"Well, okay then, thanks! What's your name?"

"Shannon, and yours?" Shannon raised an eyebrow to him as she asked. "It's Edward, but you can call me Sir if you'd like." Edward jokingly laughed as he stuck out a hand to her, offering a shake. Shannon accepted and outreached her soft hands and gave an honest shake back. Firm, but with a bit of give. "Okay, Ed...nice to meet you," she said shyly. "And you the same," Edward replied as he attempted to hide his grimace that was bound to show itself. Edward never appreciated being called Ed. He immensely disliked it. *'Just say my fucking name,'* He thought.

Shannon then winced her eyes across the table. "You know, I'm not sure if you're even old enough to talk to me, Ed; I might be a little old for you." Edward let a large smile show, exposing his teeth, once again hiding his disdain for being called Ed. "Well, you don't look old at all, Shannon, but I'm thirty. Can I ask your age? Don't be shy." Shannon hung her head laughing momentarily and then piped back up with reluctance. "You are too young for me; I'm thirty-six."

"HAH!" Edward roared back to her, his head lurching backward into a laugh. Shannon immediately reared her head back in embarrassment, regretting her honesty. Edward quickly followed, "No! No! No! I'm so sorry! I wasn't laughing at your age; I was laughing that you thought that was old!" He could sense her unease and didn't want to tarnish his chance. He sat back, convinced his last remark had saved it. After all, he was willing to forgive all the "Ed" calling.

Shannon's offense subsided a bit, letting a grin creep back. "Well, okay, I guess I believe you." Edward inserted himself again, "Besides, thirty-six isn't even old at all. Shit, you aren't even really considered old until you're...I don't know.... thirty-seven?" Shannon eased into a laughter of acceptance at Edward's poor attempt at humor. *'Okay, the date is saved,'* he remarked in his mind. He took a deep sigh of relief but concealed it from showing. There was no room for this to go south. Edward had to play the game just right to get what he wanted.

Shannon continued the conversation. "Okay, so maybe I'm not old, but you are definitely an asshole!" Shannon continued laughing, "Now, how about that drink?"

"What'll it be?"

"Whiskey sour," she replied. Edward waved his hand to grab the bartender's attention. He nodded to Edward in acknowledgment. "Um, yeah, can I get a whiskey sour and a small glass of bourbon? Jim Beam, please." The bartender produced quickly, and Edward retrieved the drinks. Shannon took a long sip and sighed, "So Ed, you from around here? Most people out here are farmers, rednecks, or wannabe cowboys, and you don't look like any of those." Edward let out a laugh, once again exposing his white smile to conceal another grimace of aversion. *There she goes again with that Ed.* "Um yeah, I'm not a farmer or a redneck... and I'm definitely not a cowboy. I grew up in the suburbs. I know, quite a bore. Suburban white boy." He threw his hands up and shrugged his shoulders, continuing, "I came out here a few years ago, though. I like the quiet and being away from everything. I bought an old house with seven acres of land off Route 614, and you?"

"Oh well, me, I was born and raised here. Never was a city gal, never will be." Shannon said this boastfully as she slammed the rest of her drink in one large gulp. Edward's eyes widened, and his eyebrows raised. "Wow, I'm impressed; the girl can handle her whiskey." Shannon let a smug grin creep onto her lips, "I can handle a lot more than that." Now, it was Edward who was blushing. "Well, can I get you another?" Shannon bit her lip and looked Edward up and down. She was obviously contemplating how the night would go, as allowing Edward to buy a second drink would send specific signals. However, it still did not promise anything. She analyzed Edward intently, deciding if he was worth the possible morning-after shame she often felt when she embarked on such nights. She let out another smile, "Sure, Hun, go for it." Edward smiled, contented. This night was going just fine.

Before long, an hour had gone by, and one drink had turned into several. The night seemed to be going well for both Edward and Shannon. Edward had a few drinks in him but was being cautious to pace himself. He wanted to be loose but needed to stay focused. Shannon, on the other hand, had no regard for pace. She had easily gulped down twice the liquor Edward had. With each drink she consumed, the more he became excited and aroused. Edward's mind was immersed in the possibilities of the night and was eager to have her, but he could not rush the process for the sake of pleasuring himself. *'Coming on too strong might be off-putting, but if she's willing, who knows...'* Edward trailed off in his own thoughts and snapped back to reality.

Before long, Edward had slid his chair around the table, sitting next to Shannon. They both took turns telling jokes and funny stories of their pasts, leaning in and bumping shoulders. After the initial awkwardness of the night was gone and both seemed well and comfortable, Edward went in for the kill. "You know, the tab here is starting to get a little high; we could always take this back to my place and drink on the house. I got a bottle of Wild Turkey on the shelf." Edward was filled with angst as he attempted to read her face and awaited a reply. Shannon cocked her head to the side and expressed an 'ah-ha' look at Edward's attempt to swoon her. "Ah well, I guess in that case, we better get going, Ed. Are you good to drive? I'm sure as shit not." She let out another laugh. Edward shared a laugh with her through the antipathy.

Edward was almost baffled by her answer. As soon as the words left his mouth, he feared he had shot the harpoon at the whale too soon. Not that Edward thought she looked like a whale; she was in relatively great shape. Of course, he could only envision the whole picture that would reveal itself later. Her answer gave Edward an assurance to a confidence already in abundance.

"Umm... yeah, sure, I kind of expected you to put up more of a fight; that was fast." Edward shrugged in agreement.

"Hey, just as long as you aren't fast, we'll get along just fine." Shannon gave Edward a wink and continued, "Besides, at my age, when you know what you want, you just take it. I'm too old to play hard to get." Edward chuckled and then pulled out his phone as if he were checking something but had no intention of doing so. Shannon couldn't tell if he was checking the time or perhaps reading a text. Maybe another girl he had met here? Oh well, she told herself. None of that mattered now.

"Well, I'll tell you what," Edward replied as he looked back and forth between his phone and her. He continued, "I got my truck parked out front, a black '89 Ford;

why don't you go ahead and wait by it? I just gotta make a phone call really quick. Be out in just a minute if you don't mind." The look in his eyes would give a person the impression that it wasn't a suggestion, but Shannon was far too drunk to notice.

Shannon stood up from her chair and stretched her back. "Sure, Hun, just don't take too long; you don't want this old lady drying up on ya." Edward almost winced at this comment, pursing his lips out and lowering his eyebrows as he thought on it for a second, then quickly shook his head in a "whatever" fashion. Shannon gathered her purse, sipped the last drops from her previous drink, and walked out. The bartender who was wiping down the bar top glanced up at her and then quickly turned his attention back to his work. Edward sat there and waited for a few moments. He mindlessly scrolled on his phone, paying it no mind. He glanced back and forth between his screen and the bartender until he was sure the bartender had seen that he was now alone.

About four minutes passed before he noticed the barkeep look over to him, who paid him minimal attention. *'Now's perfect,'* he said to himself. He then stood up and lingered for a moment. As he began to walk out, he took a few extra steps to walk up by the bar. As his movement approached the bar, he caught the barkeep's attention again, just as he intended. Edward made eye contact with him and shrugged his shoulders with his mouth in a slant, "Guess I struck out tonight," and then continued walking out the door. The bartender smirked but didn't miss a beat in what was already occupying his attention. For Edward, the foundation was set.

Edward walked out to find Shannon leaning against his pick-up. In an exaggerated motion, she looked at a non-existent watch on her wrist, "What took so long? You trying to get an extra chick to bring home with you too? Cuz I don't share," she said. She quickly raised one eyebrow and added, "Unless you're into that, then maybe I do." She let out a horrendous drunken laugh. Edward walked to the driver's side of the truck and looked at her in the darkness over the hood, "Oh, nothing dear, just making sure the stars are aligned." A drunken Shannon laughed, "Whatever that means, let's get out of here." But for Edward, the stars had aligned just perfectly for him tonight. *'Poor girl, lucky me.'* He thought as he looked her up and down one last time under the darkness. Both climbed into the truck. Edward started it up with the same low roar from earlier in the evening and drove out of the lot.

Chapter 5

It took Edward almost twenty minutes to return home from the bar. He swung into his driveway, which ran close to four hundred feet to where he parked his truck next to the pole barn. Coasting down the bumpy drive, Shannon broke the silence, "Looks like you forgot to leave the light on, can't see shit out here." Edward noticed that her southern-country accent was becoming slightly southern-trash with the effects of the booze. He didn't mind much; Edward kind of liked trashy women. A flashing image of Edward's uncle Dave popped into his head saying, 'ain't *nothin' hotter than taking a poor girl home to fuck 'er in 'er trailer.'* Dave was a unique man but stepped in as a father to Edward and his sister growing up. Edward's father split before he could remember. Just a floating memory or two of him left. Dave had taken care of him and Elaine after their mother's death. Edward snapped out of his wandering mind.

"It's not so bad once your eyes adjust; the moon lights it up nice some nights." Edward swung the truck into its usual spot and stomped the parking brake pedal to the floor. He cut the engine off and asked Shannon, "Shall we?" "We shall!" Shannon drunkenly giggled. They exited the vehicle and walked to the house, carefully finding their steps in the dark. Shannon looked at the sky as they approached the porch, nearly losing her step. "Sky sure is beautiful out here, ain't it?" Edward looked up at the clear sky, abundantly filled with stars. "Yeah, you can see Jupiter most nights." Shannon let out a "humph" and nothing more.

Edward stuck in the key, turned, and pushed the door open. They went inside, and Edward flicked on the light. The room lit up and revealed pleasant country décor.

Shannon's eyes wandered in amazement, "Wow, you decorate yourself?"

"Yeah... took a while to figure out what looked good and what didn't. Got a whole shed of ugly decorations if you want them."

"My house has enough junk already, but thanks." She let out a huffing chuckle. Her eyes then fixed on the fireplace. "That's a lovely mantel, that come with the house?" Edward walked up next to her side, staring at it with her. He slipped an arm around her tiny waist; she didn't seem to mind. "No, it's an antique one that someone was selling. I didn't like the wood engravings on the original as much as I liked this one, so I ripped out the old one and then mounted this one. It was painted originally, but I stripped it down and stained it to restore it to its old glory." Shannon pursed her lips together and raised her eyebrows in admiration. "Wow, I'm impressed! Good looking and handy."

"I don't know about either of those, but I'll surely take the compliment." Shannon and Edward's faces turned to each other. Shannon smiled and spoke again. "So, do I get another drink? Or did you strictly bring me here to take advantage of me?" Edward chuckled and began walking towards the dining room, where his liquor cabinet rested.

"Oh, don't worry, I'm quite the gentleman." Still facing the mantel, Shannon turned her head over her shoulder as Edward walked away, "Hey, I didn't say that you *couldn't* take advantage of me, but when a lady is promised free drinks on the house, she's gonna get free drinks on the house! Gotta take advantage, myself." Edward let out a smile, thinking of his night ahead. Now that she was here, he could barely contain his excitement but put on a game face. "Now, I don't have the stuff to make you a whiskey sour, or the skills for that matter, but I can make you a whiskey plain..." He trailed off with an eccentric enthusiasm. Shannon shouted from the other room, "That'll do just fine, Hun, just toss some ice into it."

Edward trotted into the kitchen and flung open the freezer door. He reached in, grabbed a few cubes from the ice maker, and splashed them into the glass. He walked back to the living room and handed over the glass. "Sorry, I don't have any of that fancy bar ice." She took it from him and immediately took a swig. "Thanks, Hun, this will do just fine. Nothing for you?" Edward held his hand up and shook his head, "No, I like to keep my mind clear. Can I show you the tour?"

"Why, of course, Ed, how gentlemanly of you."
Edward then held out his hand in a motion for her to lead
him into the kitchen as he held back another cringe from
being called Ed again. She began to walk and look at the
room. He then pointed to a door on the other side of the
kitchen, "That's the den. I've got a few projects going on;
you should take a peek." Edward held his hand out, with the
palm facing up in a 'please proceed' manner.

"I guess I shall," she replied as she gave a half curtsy
to him in a joking manner. She began to head there slowly,
eyes still gazing around the room. As she walked away,
Edward's face turned to his right, and he looked at a black
metal candle sconce hanging on the wall. He quickly glanced
back at Shannon, who was paying him no mind. She was too
busy admiring the rustic tone of the house. Edward reached
up and planted his right palm on the plaster wall just above
the sconce, feeling the roughness of the deteriorating paint.
He slowly slid it down the uneven plaster until his hand
covered the sconce. He grabbed it gently off the wall,
lowered it behind his back, and began to follow Shannon. A

few loose paint chips flaked off onto the floor, leaving small exposures of rust on the bare metal.

She opened the door and walked into the dark room. As she walked in, she felt and heard what sounded like a tarp beneath her feet. She audibly searched for a light switch a few seconds before the light snapped on. Sure enough, as she looked down, clear and blue plastic tarps were lying on the floor. "What's with all this shit, Ed?" she asked as she was looking down, stepping on the loose bulges in the plastic. Edward walked up slowly behind her, "Oh, I'm actually about to do some painting in here." Edward slowly brought the sconce around his mid-section and met it with his other hand. He stood there with his hands at the base of it, holding it in front of him, carrying it as a bride would her bouquet walking down the aisle. "Oh yeah?" She asked with what seemed genuine curiosity, "What color?"

"I was thinking red?" Edward answered with a smirk. He struggled to hold back but let out a laugh, covering his mouth. He lowered his left hand off the sconce to his side. "Red? That's a little bold for a room, don't you think, Ed......" Edward calmed his voice into a serious, almost condescending tone, "You know, you really should stop calling me that." Edward giggled his way through his entire remark. "Calling you wha..."

Before finishing her sentence, Edward walked quickly behind her, reared the sconce high above his head, and brought it down with all his strength to the back of her skull like a lumberjack attempting to split a log in one swing. Contact was made with the cracking sound of a bludgeoning blow, instantly fracturing her cranium and producing a large blood splatter. Her head slumped forward, and her body went limp before it even began to topple over to the floor. The thud of her body hitting the floor followed just a second later.

Edward looked at the walls and saw the immense splatter running down and soaking in the white paint. "SHIT!" he screamed in anger. He looked down at Shannon's pathetic, limp body lying lazily on the floor. Like the town drunk after a fifth of whiskey. His blood was boiling. She began to moan and squirmed like an earthworm on a hot sidewalk, unable to speak. He looked at the walls again and followed the blood streams down to the baseboards. Now, in a fit of rage, he got down to his knees and straddled her body. Although moving and moaning, he was unsure if any cognitive intelligence was left in there. He rolled her to her back and grabbed her face, turning it towards the blood-splattered wall. "LOOK WHAT YOU DID, YOU STUPID BITCH!" He shouted with everything he had inside him, spitting as the words flew from his lips. He looked up at the wall for a third time and then shot his attention quickly back to her. His breathing was heavy at first but calmed rapidly. He took several long, deep breaths until he could feel his heart rate lower and his anger simmer.

He slid his hand down her face to her throat, where it was joined by the other. He began to squeeze but then backed off. He looked down at himself, unbuckled his belt, and slid it out from the loops. He reached down and slid it under the nape of her neck. Once wrapped around it, he put it through the metal loop on the buckle and cinched it down with force. Shannon's eyes opened, and her body began to flail rapidly. She was starting to regain some form of consciousness, but Edward was unsure how lucid she was. Edward stared into her eyes. He could see fear and confusion. It was clear she had no knowledge of how she got in this position from just speaking a moment before. He ripped the long end of the belt up towards his face, causing her head to snatch from the floor. A croak of wind emitted from her mouth. A small but steady stream of blood ran from her head to the tile like a trickle of a creek running over a rock. Edward reached out, placed his left hand on her forehead, and thrust it back to the floor surface, keeping a taut hold on the belt to maintain pressure. Shannon's eyes began to roll up and then abruptly stopped. Her body lay there motionless, but her eyes remained open. Edward stared into them for a few moments. Dark and lifeless; dead man's eyes, as Edward referred to them. Shannon was dead. The hard part was over, but much work was still ahead of him.

Edward walked over to the kitchen counter and retrieved his headphones. He slid in each earbud and then scrolled through a list of songs on his phone's playlist. Once he came to a choice, he returned the phone to his pocket. He stood there momentarily and closed his eyes as the music began to play. He began to hum to the violin and moved his hand back and forth in front of him as if he were a Maestro conducting a symphony. He opened his eyes and looked back at Shannon on the floor. He slowly walked over and knelt in front of her. *'Making love is always better than the sound of music,'* he recited.

Edward unbuttoned Shannon's jeans and slid the zipper down to the bottom, exposing her black lace underwear. Edward reached down, inserted his right index finger into the band at the top, and moved it back and forth, rubbing her soft skin where her stomach met the pelvic region. He quickly retreated his hand and then grabbed the jean's waistline on her hips and began to yank them down. His hands then ran down her pant legs and used a tight grasp on the ankle cuffs to finish removing the clothing. Edward then quickly pulled Shannon's underpants. He slid her t-shirt up to the base of her breasts and then spread her legs to expose her vagina.

Edward placed his left hand on her stomach, hiding the naval. He then took his right hand and slid his fingers up the inside of her right thigh and then circled her labia. Edward could feel an erection forming in his pants. After a moment, he slid his first two fingers inside of her. She was still warm and wet inside. He then placed his thumb on her clitoris. He immediately looked up at Shannon's face, almost expecting to see some expression of gratification or arousal from her. Shannon's eyes continued to stare at the ceiling, dark and lifeless. Edward continued to massage the inside of Shannon with his fingertips for a few more moments and then pulled them out. He looked at the thin fluid layer on his fingertips and inserted them into his mouth. Edward closed his eyes as he tasted her. *'What a sweet-tasting woman...at least she tastes young,'* Edward thought. He swirled his tongue around his fingers in his mouth, licking up every drop of her off his skin. He pulled his fingers from his lips and swirled his tongue around the inside of his mouth once more and then swallowed. *'All gone.'*

Edward had a full erection now. He was throbbing and could feel semen begin to ooze out of the tip of his penis. He quickly reached into his back-right pocket to retrieve his wallet and fumbled inside until he found a condom. Edward always kept one inside. He tore open the wrapper and slid the condom down to the base of his penis. He positioned himself between her legs to mount her and then slid himself inside as far as he could. As he thrust himself inside over and over, he leaned down to kiss her lips. They were still warm but felt dry and stiff. He then turned her head to her right, exposing her left cheek to him. He leaned in once again and placed his tongue on her jawline. He proceeded to drag his tongue up her bloody cheek, making complete contact with the surface of it. As his tongue retreated back into his mouth, he could taste the iron in her blood.

Edward pulled her shirt the rest of the way up to expose her breasts. He placed the left breast inside his mouth and began to suck on it as he thrust himself even harder. Edward began to feel himself reach the point of no return. Then he thrust himself as hard as he could, holding a tight grip of her breast in his mouth as he felt a full release of semen shoot out of him, filling up the condom still inside of her. He continued to thrust himself into her several more times, ensuring to empty himself inside of her warm body.

He was out of breath. *'a good fuck always gets you.'* He said in his head. He lay on top of her, panting for a full minute, and then slid out of her, still holding the base of the condom so that it didn't remove itself in her tight sheath. Edward pulled the condom off and threw it in the trash. He then retrieved a paper towel from the counter to clean himself off. As he wiped himself, he looked down at her in displeasure as if her body had already gone putrid. He looked at her head to see a profusion of blood leaking from it. *'What a disgusting cunt.'* After disposing of the towel, he pushed his penis back in through his zipper and pulled it up.

Edward undressed the rest of Shannon's body. He put the clothes in his arms and placed them in a chair in the kitchen at a small table nook. He then stepped over her body and stood between her head and the back door of the house. Exhausted from his escapade, he let out an overwhelming sigh. He knew it was time to clean up. It was not a part he was particularly fond of, but it was essential- a necessary evil he liked to think of it.

He bent over and grabbed a fist full of her hair. Edward began to wrap her hair around his grip, winding it into a tight ball around his fist. Edward extended his left hand just far enough to the back door and turned the knob. He exited the house still with a tight grab of Shannon's hair. He could almost hear her scalp stretching as he pulled her through the doorway. Similar to a tanner trying a piece of leather to be cured. He then went down the back-stoop stairs with her departed body dragging behind him. Shannon's body thumping down the wooden steps one by one echoed throughout the backyard, but no one would hear.

Edward dragged her around the side of the house and then dropped her head, letting it whack against the ground like a giant rock. Edward then walked to the hose spigot and opened it all the way. He began to unwind the hose until enough slack reached the body. He threw the lead of the hose over his shoulder and walked to Shannon. He looked down at her filthy and perverted body. Dirt clung to every blood spot on her skin, turning it to a murky red-brown mud. Edward looked into her cold, dead eyes, 'Pathetic.' He then turned the hose to her, squeezed the handle on the nozzle, and began to wash her. He started with her head, holding the stream steady on her face for a moment, making it disappear behind a miniature waterfall. Edward needed to wash the filth off her, the squalidness out of her. He moved the stream of water down her body, washing her clean.

After he was done, Edward pulled a set of leather gloves from his pocket and slid them on his hands. He wrapped his hand again in her hair and dragged her back through the dirt. This time, he went around the front of the house to the bed of his truck. He returned to the house and removed the tarp on the floor where Shannon had fallen. He gathered it up and took it back to her body. He spread it out on the grass next to her lifeless body and rolled her up inside. He grabbed the tightly packaged body and threw it into the truck bed. Edward hopped in and drove off the property.

Twelve miles from his home, Edward pulled into a field and drove about two hundred feet from the road. There stood a large oak tree with a solid trunk. Edward grabbed an old rope from underneath the bench seat and hopped out. He strutted through the tall, knee-high grass to the base of the trunk and tossed the rope onto the ground, then went back to retrieve Shannon. Edward threw her tarp-wrapped body over his shoulder. She was getting stiffer but not fully rigor mortis yet.

As he brought her over, he lay her body down and unrolled the tarp. He once again stood over her, observing her naked body. He then took the extra slack of the rope and tied it into a slipknot around her neck. Once it was pulled taut, he dragged her underneath a branch and launched the slack of the rope over. There was just enough hanging on the other side to jump up and grasp it. He took the slack and quickly ran around the base of the tree with it while struggling to hold Shannon's weight. Once around, he tied the rope off on itself.

There she hung, dangling in the night, her pale body illuminated by the moon. Edward pulled out a four-inch pocket knife and opened the blade. He steadied her body and then began to carve into her soft stomach flesh. Dead blood began to slowly seep from the opening he created. He made the marks he needed and then returned to review his work. Edward was satisfied with the outcome of her conclusion. Edward walked back to the truck and hopped in. He took one last good look at Shannon through the windshield. "Goodbye, Hun," he said to her through the glass in her stupid country accent. He fired the engine up and turned the truck around. Edward drove to the main road through the field and headed home.

Chapter 6

"Please, give me something here…" Detective Bradley pleaded to an agitated forensic scientist on the other end. He continued, "It's been over two months since we sent you our first samples and almost a month since our last!" A huff came over the line, followed by an annoyed forty-something-year-old woman's voice. "Detective, I understand your frustration, but these things take time, sometimes several months. We're backlogged thousands of cases across the state, and certain cases take preced…" "Precedence?" Detective Bradley quickly cut her off, almost laughing to keep himself from blowing a gasket. Detective Bradley never backed down from calling someone out on something he felt was utter bullshit.

"Precedence? Ma'am, I've got three dead women, young girls... that I know of. There could be a dozen more, and I have nothing to go off. I know they were all killed by the same man, but I need you to help me prove it." Another sigh came over the line, but this time, it seemed less of an annoyed sigh and more of an understanding one. "Look, Detective, I get it...you're passionate about what you're doing, as you should be, but we still have other cases we must also give attention to." Her voice broke away from the phone as Detective Bradley could hear the rustling of papers. She returned, "Now, I'm not supposed to release any results until the final analysis is typed up, but I can talk to you on the low if you can pretend this conversation never happened."

"Absolutely," Michael quickly replied. There was a slight pause before she spoke again. "The first two girls, Miss Robinson and Miss Vermond... we got nothing. All the blood and fluid samples we analyzed belonged to each girl. We're only halfway through the samples with Miss Shire, but..."

"But what?" Detective Bradley asked hastily. She finished, "but it's not looking good." Michael reached up with his left hand and massaged both sides of his temple. He let out a large sigh, "Okay... thanks for that," Michael said sincerely.

Michael was genuinely grateful that she gave him an honest answer to his inquiry about the situation. However, he still found it hard to be thankful for this situation in general.

"No problem, just remember you didn't get that info from me. The letters with the official results will be finished by tomorrow and should be in your office by next week. Make sure that's where you got your information from." Michael looked down at his dingy dress shoes while tapping his foot against the floor, "Of course... and can I get your name, ma'am?"

"Melissa Madson. If you have any more questions or concerns, you can just ask for me."

"Thank you, ma'am, I'll be in touch." As Michael ended his conversation, Detective Lugo was arriving for the day. He slowly walked over and placed his suit coat on the rack beside his desk. He plopped down into his chair and stared at Michael. Michael hung up the phone and threw his head back, looking at the ceiling. He then shook his head back and forth as if shaking out some lousy thought. Detective Lugo slid down in his chair, stretching his legs out in front of him and crossing his hands on his lap. "I guess that answers my question on if you heard anything back from the state lab."

Detective Bradley looked towards Daniel, chewing his lower lip, "Nothing on the first two girls, still working on the third... probably nothing there either."

"Well, shit..." Daniel looked up at the whiteboard with all their notes, hoping to jog his memory for a new idea, although he knew it wouldn't work. "We can go back and question friends and family again; see if we missed anything." Michael shrugged his shoulders and tossed his hands up a few inches out of his lap, "What for? Nobody gave us shit, nobody knew anything. I don't think our guy had any personal connection to any of these girls. Besides, we spent close to forty hours' worth of interviews per victim, and nobody gave us fucking shit to go off of." Michael's tone became increasingly angrier as his statement went on. Daniel rocked back further in his chair. He kicked his legs up on his desk and interlocked his fingers behind his head. "So where do we go from here?" Detective Bradley leaned over his desk and rested his face in his left hand, "I don't fuckin' know, man."

Chapter 7

As Monday progressed, the late afternoon was met with a somber orange glow covering the town. Edward was putting on a nice three-piece suit upstairs in his bedroom. Edward dressed up infrequently. He didn't care to look fancy to anyone; however, these events often called for a particular dress code. He figured if he must, he must do it in proper fashion. Edward has had this suit for years but was quite fond of it. He was a big fan of having the vest piece under the jacket. He felt it added a certain sophisticated edge to the look.

He would be making the two-hour drive to Richmond to see a local community-style symphony in just a bit. Usually filled with self-taught musicians and some that played through high school and college, they still put on a hell of a show, and the tickets were dirt cheap. Edward was a sincere fan of classical music since he was a teenager. Tonight, the symphony was doing a rendition of Tchaikovsky's "The Nutcracker." It was one of Edward's favorite pieces. Edward remembered his third-grade music teacher showing a video at Christmas of the piece, a play of sorts, he thought, but couldn't quite recall everything. He only remembered giant Nutcracker costumes and ballet dancers prancing around the stage. Although not a fan of the play, he found himself delighted with the music, even at such a young age.

The show didn't begin until nine, but Edward liked taking advantage of the pleasant evening to go into the city for drinks and a cordial dinner. He had an appointment with his counselor, Dr. Brown, in less than an hour, but Edward would not be appearing for that. A special night like tonight could not be wasted sitting on an old couch to speak about his feelings. He would undoubtedly make it a point to be present for the next one.

Edward tied his four-in-hand knot in his tie and then looked at himself in the mirror mounted atop his dresser. He was impressed with his look: a black pinstripe coat, vest, and pants, with a navy blue shirt with a black tie and silver clasp. Edward could not find the matching cuff links, but he was too excited about his evening to care. No eyes would be on him. All eyes would be glued to the show at hand. He went to the bathroom to comb his hair, splashed a spray of cologne, and then left the house. Walking to the truck, he took in a breath of refreshing country air. He listened to some of his other favorite classical pieces to set the mood, but not The Nutcracker. He didn't want to spoil the evening. After his hard work, he felt he deserved the time to relax and recuperate. This night was a special treat for him. Edward climbed into his truck and set off on his drive.

<u>Chapter 8</u>

Just after nine in the evening, as Edward's show was just beginning, Detective Michael Bradley was lounging in an old brown leather recliner in front of the television. Although extremely tired and knowing that a good night's sleep was much needed for his physical and mental health, Michael decided that beer and Monday night football were better options for stress relief. Something about a dark lager and watching two-hundred-pound men hit each other like freight trains always put him in a better mood.

It was only the beginning of the second quarter, and Michael was halfway through a bag of chips and almost a whole jar of salsa. Those two things never disappeared at an equal pace. Michael leaned over to the end table to his right when he felt his phone vibrate in his pocket. He tossed the bowl on the tabletop and quickly retrieved the phone. It was Daniel's name showing on the screen. Not really in the mood to talk, Michael began to place the phone down on the arm of the chair when he hesitated. Something inside told him it wasn't just a call from a friend at this time of night. Michael decided to answer. "Hey brother, what's up?" Michael barely got the words out of his mouth before Daniel shot through with a more than serious tone, "Hey, get dressed! They just found another body." An extreme hot flash immediately shot through Michael's body, and his skin was instantly populated with bumps and raised hair. "Fuck! Where at?" He shouted back into the phone. Daniel replied, "Iverson farm, his back forty behind the corn fields. Head down south on Route 32 from Main, and you'll find it.

Apparently, it's already a shit show out there. I'm leaving now; hurry."

"Got it," Michael said back to Daniel. He wasn't sure if he got it out before Daniel hung up on his end, but that didn't matter. Michael got dressed in celebrity and grabbed his badge and gun on the way out.

Only twenty minutes passed before Michael pulled up to the scene. He could instantly sense the chaos around him. There were emergency lights everywhere. "Who the fuck are all these people?" He said out loud to himself in his car. There were at least a dozen police cruisers on scene. Usually, this would raise suspicion, as there were just over fifty officers on Emerald's payroll, but he immediately knew why. All of Emerald's police cruisers bared both blue and red lights, whereas the Virginia State Police cruisers only used blue. All but three of the cruisers on scene showed nothing but blue. "Fucking Troopers." Michael once again voiced to himself inside the car. He parked behind the lone ambulance on scene. It was protocol to have EMS arrive on scene even if it was known the victim was already dead before their arrival.

Detective Lugo had beaten him to the scene. Michael hopped out and met Daniel in the field on the other side of the road. He could see a group of officers and troopers about two hundred to two hundred fifty feet into the field from the road, all gathered around a tree. "What the fuck is up with all the Staties?" Michael shouted to Daniel as he approached his position. Daniel threw his hands up from his side, "Take a guess."

"They aren't taking this fucking investigation from us. Now, all of a sudden, they care?" Daniel just stared back at him for a moment before responding. "Let's walk and talk; they're like vultures on a dead deer over there." They both started strutting through the high grass to the body. Michael asked Daniel, "So what do we know so far?" Daniel sighed as he responded, "Umm... well, Randall Iverson, the property owner, found her. He was riding his tractor through the field and saw some buzzards flying around. He figured a dead animal was in the field, so he went looking. Didn't even see her hanging there at first.... I almost drove right past her. Name's Shannon Reed." Michael's eyebrows raised in amazement, "We got an ID already?"

"Yeah... Iverson knew who she was as soon as he saw her. Said they went to church together. Poor fuck puked everywhere." Michael quickly shot his face back over to Daniel with concern. Daniel quickly identified his fear, "Don't worry, he was smart… held it in until he was far enough away, no contamination."

"What about a message? Anything?" Michael asked. It was just then that they were coming up on the body. Daniel pointed to Shannon, still dangling from the rope and slightly swaying in the breeze, "See for yourself." Michael looked up at Shannon and observed numerous lacerations to her stomach. Just a split second later, he realized the cuts were the message. Carved into Shannon's body from just under the bottom of her breasts to her pelvic region were the words "SHE DANCED THE DANCE OF DEATH."

A grim aura shadowed the girl's body, like a scene from hell itself. Michael couldn't comprehend the mindset a man would have to be in to do this to an innocent woman. "Jesus fuck man, what's wrong with this guy?" Daniel didn't respond. They both began looking around the scene. Everyone seemed to be pretending to be busier than they were. No one wanted to be the guy standing around doing nothing on an incident like this. Not only was it not a good time to appear lazy, but if a Sergeant caught an officer doing nothing, he was sure to pass out some bullshit tasks to avoid a Lieutenant shitting down the Sergeant's neck about the officers standing around with their thumbs up their asses. Michael broke the silence again, "So, who's in charge of the Troopers over here?" Daniel pointed to the lot of them, "There was a sergeant walking around, but I'm pretty sure I saw a lieutenant at one point, too. I'm sure he can tell us who is if he's not."

Both detectives walked over and found the Lieutenant amongst his Trooper gathering. Detective Lugo piped up over the coffee talk and laughs among them, "Sir, could we borrow you for a moment?" The Lieutenant gave his men and woman a nod and told them he would be back in a moment. Detective Lugo and Bradley walked away from the group to hint for the LT to follow. Once away, Detective Bradley took no time to bring up his concerns. "Look, sir. We appreciate all your help out here tonight, but with all due respect, this is our case. We've already begun..."
"Hold up right there, brother." The LT held his hand up to Michael as a gesture to halt and then continued. "We don't want any part of this shit; you can keep it. We just heard the radio call come out. We figured we'd lend a hand to help

secure a perimeter for y'all and maybe do some canvass interviews or something if you need us to. This is still all you."

Michael and Daniel both let out a sigh of relief. They knew in the end, if the state wanted the investigation, they would get it. Too much bureaucracy involved and saving public face over the lack of resources that were at hand to catch this guy. The State Police would never take an investigation from a larger department. Still, with Emerald's small stature, it was a concern. Daniel gave him a nod, "Thank you, sir, we appreciate the help." The LT nodded in acknowledgment, "No problem, we'll leave our forensic investigators out here to assist yours in collecting evidence; maybe save you a few hours of work." A cross of 'thanks' was given, followed by an exchange of handshakes before they parted ways.

Daniel began walking back towards the chaos. "I know a beat officer already spoke with Iverson, but I guess we should as well."
"For sure. Hopefully, he's all there for us. I'm sure this is quite the mind fuck. Could you imagine finding this shit on

your own property?" Michael asked rhetorically. Both walked over to him, sitting on the ground, almost hidden in the high grass. Iverson knew they were coming to question him and stood up to greet them both with a shake. "Mr. Iverson," Daniel announced, "I know an officer probably questioned you already, but I'm sure you know how this stuff goes."

"Yeah, absolutely; I know you gotta do whatcha gotta do." Daniel continued to kick off the questioning. "So, can you go back over how you found her?"

"Sure," Iverson responded. "I was riding my tractor out from the cow pasture to the stalls. I have to go around the corn fields so I don't plow over the crops. As I approached the stalls, I saw a swarm of buzzards, vultures, or whatever have you... thought maybe a deer got hit and ran into the field and died or something; it happens sometimes. Anyways, they kept flyin' around that tree right there, but I was looking for something on the ground and didn't even see her at first. By the time I realized what was there, I was frozen solid."

"What then?" Daniel asked. Well, I walked up to her.... I didn't know what else to do right then. I didn't touch her, though; I knew she was gone. I ran back over to the house and called the law from there." This time, Michael asked a question: "We were told you know her. Is that true?"

"Yeah, I do; we go to First Baptist in town. Talk to her from time to time, real sweet girl. Never seen anyone like that before..." He trailed off briefly before continuing, "No life in the face like that, no life in the eyes. Just staring right at you." Michael didn't lend any coping time in true cop fashion. "I know this is hard for you, sir. Do you know if she has any family here in town?" Iverson snapped out of a dead stare. "Her parents are dead, but she did have a roommate. She lived in the Grammar Apartments just outside of the town. Couldn't give you a phone number or apartment number, sorry."

"That's alright, we'll take care of all that," Michael said back to him. "When was the last time you rode through here? At least, when you would have noticed she wasn't here." Iverson thought about it a minute before answering. "Five days, I guess, maybe a week. I don't come this far back often. Sorry, that's the best I can give you." Daniel leaned over and spoke softly to Michael, "She still looks decently fresh. I don't think she's been out here that long." Michael nodded in agreement. "Alright, Mr. Iverson, we appreciate your help; I know you don't have too much to give. If you think of anything else, just give us a call. And if we need anything else from you, we'll do the same. I believe the uniform officer got all of your information." Daniel reached out and handed him a business card, and then both detectives walked back to where Shannon was still hanging.

The forensic investigators and a representative from the state Medical Examiner's office were still near the body. "Do we know how long she's been here yet?" Michael asked no one in particular. The medical examiner representative piped up first, "Based on temperature and the absence of body decay, I'd say she's been dead between eighteen and twenty-four hours." Daniel looked over to Michael, "Shit, he was just here." Michael didn't acknowledge Daniel's statement, but his expression as he gazed over Shannon's body made it clear he was thinking the same thing. Michael snapped out of his stare and made eye contact with the medical examiner's office representative. "Anything gathered that gives us anything?" She shrugged her shoulders, "Hard to say; she's covered in dirt, but her hair was still damp. It didn't rain yesterday, so she must have been washed at some point. I think all the mud helped keep the moisture in it this long."

"Wet hair." Michael stated to himself out loud and then looked over to Daniel, "Same as the others; I think he's hosing them down or bathing them." Daniel looked up as he pondered the statement. "Hosing is easier, bathing is more thorough…, but he's doing something to cover himself as far as DNA." The medical examiner rep began packing up her kit. "We've done all we can here; we'll need to get her back to the office and let the medical examiner do her thing. Once she's there, we'll hit her with the UV light and see if there are any fluids on her to test that might not be hers."

"Great," Daniel stated as he pointed back towards the road. Michael looked over and saw two local news channel vans approaching the scene. "Well, that didn't take long," he responded to Daniel. Daniel shook his head in annoyance, "Ah yes, the real vultures. Anything for ratings, it seems," He paused momentarily. "It's those fucking scanners. That's what happens when the department won't shell out the cash for an encrypted radio system." Michael turned his head away from the road and focused his attention back on Shannon, looking her up and down one last time. He said something of a prayer for her in his mind, hoping she was in a better place. Hell, any place was better than how she was left and went out. He then looked over to the forensic investigators and nodded his head towards the body. "Cut her down."

Chapter 9

Edward returned home after midnight from the show. He was quite pleased with the performance. Although he could pick out a few squeaks from a third or fourth-chair violinist, it was one hell of a rendition. Edward had ripped off his tie and unbuttoned his collar when he left the venue, but he still needed to undress from his suit. Although a lovely fabric, it was not one for breathing, and he had started to sweat through the jacket by the end of the show's first piece.

He walked upstairs to his bedroom and turned on the television as he undressed. He flipped to the local Richmond news station, hoping to hear the results of the Monday night football game. Edward looked forward to the symphony so much that he couldn't even remember who had played. Although it had aired hours earlier, they usually put it on repeat a time or two into the morning hours for the night owls.

Edward had just taken off his jacket and button-up shirt when he heard the music clip that was always played for the "breaking news" section. A middle-aged female anchor was on tonight. She was pretty for her age but obviously had work done, which did not suit her well. The camera was only on her briefly before she started her segment. "Tonight, Emerald County and Virginia State Police recovered a fourth body in what they believe to be a related string of murders." The part of Edward's brain telling him to undress as he watched T.V. immediately shut off as his attention honed in on her voice. She continued with her segment, "Reports state that a local farmer found the body hanging from a tree on his property. Police have not released any information on the victim, and it is unclear if she has been identified. Ken Rogers is on scene now with Lieutenant Kelly from Virginia State Police with a statement."

The camera changed to an all-too-familiar scene. One Edward remembered being at just the night before. The first thing Edward noticed was a large white text at the bottom of the screen that read "Previously Recorded" to let everyone know it wasn't currently live anymore. Edward's focus faded to his thoughts as the on-site reporter began questioning the lieutenant. *'That was fucking quick. It was usually a few days before they were found. Was I sloppy? Did I make other mistakes? Now the State Police are involved?'* Edward was confused by his own thoughts. After all, he wanted her to be found; That was the plan. It wasn't that he didn't want her found; he was just caught off guard by how nervous he felt that she was. Edward hadn't gotten nervous before when the others were found. He didn't like the feeling. Edward didn't want to be bothered by it anymore. It was late, and he had to work the next day.

Edward climbed into the bed and tried to shut off his mind but was bothered about keeping his game going without getting caught. It wasn't about staying hidden anymore. It wasn't about the police at all. This was about Edward. This was about his urges. This was about his need. A need that no one could understand but him. Edward was confident that if ever caught, he would be poked and prodded by every doctor and psychologist on the East Coast. Trying to put some sort of label or diagnosis on him for what he's done. Edward himself didn't even understand the reason behind his grand presentation of the bodies after he was done with them. It wasn't about gaining notoriety. He just needed to share the beauty of it all with everyone. The beauty that he shared with the girls. The beauty they produced together. Edward once again shut his eyes and turned off his brain. He stared into the darkness of his eyelids and watched the figures of light dance and morph themselves into nothingness. Before long, sleep.

Chapter 10

By Tuesday afternoon, Detectives Lugo and Bradley had Shannon's address and her roommate's name. The media caught wind of Shannon's identity and plastered it all over their morning segment. There was no doubt that her roommate had already heard the news. The detectives parked outside the apartment building on the street and approached the door. They gave a few knocks and waited.

It was just a moment before a late thirty-something blonde came to the door. It was apparent she had been crying and was currently clutching a tissue in her left hand. Michael raised his hand and waved half-heartedly, "Charlene Harris?" Charlene nodded and began sobbing hysterically. "Ah, shit." Daniel blurted out loud. His eyes shot wide open, and he looked up to Charlene and Michael as he realized that statement probably came out louder than it should have. Daniel never did well with other people's emotions, especially sobbing. It wasn't apathy of the situation but rather a lack of knowledge of how to proceed comfortably for them. Charlene didn't register what he had said; however, Michael looked at him with his mouth stretching straight across his face while slowly shaking his head. Michael adverted his attention back to the distraught woman, "Miss Harris, do you mind if we come in and talk? It might be easier if you're sitting down." Charlene just nodded as she turned away and walked inside, leaving the door ajar. Both detectives followed and shut the door behind them.

They all entered the living room. Numerous pictures on the wall, mantel, and other shelves showed Shannon and Charlene together, along with others. Once they were all seated, Daniel kicked off the conversation. "Charlene, I know this is gonna be hard for you…. There is never enough time in the world to fully grieve the loss of a loved one; it just gets a little easier in time. I know the last thing you want to do right now is deal with the administrative bullshit and questioning of Shannon's death. Still, unfortunately, it's something that must be done." Still sobbing, Charlene nodded and gave a soft whimper, "It's okay." Daniel looked at Michael, seated beside him, and gave him a nod to start the questioning.

Michael laid a pad on his leg to write on and clicked his pen. "Ma'am, how long have you known Shannon for?" Charlene was finally able to steady her crying. Years. We were classmates in our junior year of high school. We've been best friends ever since." Michael kept the questions going. "Do you know where Shannon went when she left the house Sunday night?"

"She usually went to Benny's Tavern for a drink. That place was her favorite. The bartender always thought she was pretty, sometimes would give her drinks on the house." Michael simply wrote 'Benny's' on his notepad. "You didn't report Shannon missing. Was it common for her not to come home like that?" Charlene tilted her head back and forth, "Kinda sorta." Michael, looking confused, probed further, "I'm sorry. Can you elaborate on that?" Charlene nodded her head to comply but still wouldn't look up. "She would sometimes find a guy at the bar to go home with; she was pretty and sweet for her age. She wouldn't come home for a day or two a few times a month. I wasn't worried at first. When the news released the story last night, I had a funny feeling in my stomach, but they didn't give a name, and I just…. I never thought…." She trailed off and began crying again as she continued. "When I heard her name on the news this morning, I didn't believe it. I didn't want to believe it. I even tried calling her phone just in case." Daniel saw a box of tissues on the coffee table before him. He retrieved a new one and extended it out to Charlene. The one clutched in her hand appeared to have absorbed about as many tears and snot as possible. He decided to throw a few questions out as well.

"Charlene, you said the bartender was sweet on Shannon. Do you think he might have had something to do with this? Maybe made a pass and was upset over rejection?" Charlene looked up quickly and shook her head. "Benny? Oh God, no… That man is a sweetheart and wouldn't hurt anyone. He's never even attempted a pass at her before, and she's been drinking there for years. He knew she was a few tiers above him, and he was a gentleman about it."

"Okay," Daniel responded. "We just have to cover everything. Was there anyone she's been seeing that she might have met there? A boyfriend? Someone, she was just casually seeing?" Charlene shook her head, "No, Shannon never kept a suiter, and she wouldn't have kept one from me if she had. If I had to guess, whoever did this met her there that night." Michael added to his notes on his pad, "Do you remember what Shannon was wearing that night?" Charlene thought momentarily before answering, "Not

really, jeans and a t-shirt, likely; she wasn't a fancy girl. She
is more concerned with her comfort than her style. She was
pretty enough that she didn't need to dress nicely to get
attention. Her face and ass were all she needed." Charlene
laughed at her statement, which quickly reverted to an ugly
cry. Michael continued through the awkwardness. "So, you
said Benny was familiar with her. Would we need a picture
of her to ask if he remembers her being there on Sunday? Or
would he know her by name?" Charlene began nodding and
blowing a hard blow into her tissue, "Oh yeah, he knew her
by name, been going there every week for ten-plus years."
"Okay, great," Michael responded. Is there any other info
you could add? Anything that might help us out?"
"No, sorry…" She trailed off for a minute. "All I know is that
she was there, and then she wasn't."

Detective Lugo and Detective Bradley looked at each
other, almost asking each other with their eyes if they
should ask anything else. Usually, questioning was much
more intensive and lengthier than this, especially for such a
high-profile investigation. The only problem was that no one
seemed to know anything and had such little information to
give. Daniel stopped the eye-staring between them by

shrugging his shoulders and directed his attention back to Charlene. "Well, that's all we need to bother you with for now, ma'am. If we have any further questions for you, we will get back in touch. Also, if there is anything you have to offer, please don't hesitate to call. Any information you have could help us, no matter how unimportant it may seem." As Daniel finished his statement, he waved a business card for her to see and then placed it on the coffee table. "We'll get out of your way now and leave you to whatever you need to do. We can show ourselves out." Charlene just simply nodded her head and gave a small, pathetic smile to them.

Both detectives gathered themselves and left the apartment. As they returned to the car, Daniel instantly asked, "Straight to Benny's?" Michael replied, "Yep!" with a bit of enthusiasm. "This is the first time we have gotten a decent lead. If Benny knew her that well, there's no doubt he would have noticed someone there with her." Daniel nodded in agreement. "Shit, maybe if our guy was a regular, too, then we can get a name for him as well." Michael shrugged his shoulders, "Well, let's just see what we can get and go from there." Michael climbed into the driver's seat and started the vehicle. He took a minute to ponder the possibilities of what might be discovered at the bar and then put the car in drive and set out.

It was only ten minutes to Benny's Tavern. Michael parked the unmarked patrol car outside of the rundown brick building. The place was simply marked with a blue and red neon sign that read "Benny's Tavern." Both detectives climbed out of the vehicle and looked up at the sign. Michael looked across the top of the car at Daniel, "Have you ever actually been here before?" Still looking at the building, Daniel pursed his lips and shook his head, "Nope, driven by it a bunch, never had a desire to check it out." Michael thought about Daniel's answer and agreed, "Yeah, me neither."

They entered the bar through the front door. Both men were hit with the same aromas that Edward had experienced just two days prior. The only difference was that there was only one customer inside this time. By the looks of him, he spent most of his time here. Behind the bar was a burly-looking man with a bushy beard that was slightly greying. The bartender stared up at them as they approached. Daniel spoke out first, "Hey man, you Benny?"

"Yeah, sure am. And you?" he asked in return, as if the guns and badges on the belt weren't a big enough hint to him. "I'm Detective Lugo, and this is Detective Bradley." They both shook hands with Benny before continuing. "We were hoping you could help us with a murder from the other night." There was an instant sadness in Benny's eyes as the words left Daniel's mouth. "Shannon." He simply stated in return. "You were already expecting us then?" Daniel asked in a curious tone. Benny looked down at a rag he was winding up in his hands and then looked up at them again. "Yeah, I saw it on the news. I was gonna call you this morning, but then I figured it wouldn't be long before someone from the law showed up. Came quicker than I expected." Michael spoke up next, "So you remember her coming in here Sunday night?"
"Absolutely. She was in here every Sunday and usually Fridays, too. That girl has been coming here for over ten years."

"Do you remember if there was anybody here with her?"

"Yeah, actually, there was." This statement immediately sparked excitement in both detectives. They exchanged a hopeful eye glance at each other. Michael's excited anxiousness came through in his voice, "Do you know who he was?"

"No, sorry. Never seen him in here before, or just don't remember him at least." Daniel began looking around the bar. "Do you have any cameras in here?" Benny turned around and pointed up behind the bar, "I only got three cameras, but they won't be of any help. They're all pointed at the register and the safe, sorry." Michael huffed in annoyance, "What about outside, anything?" Benny also shook his head to that, "Nothing outside either, but I think I may have seen his truck." This especially struck the interest of both detectives. They both stared intently, waiting for him to continue with that statement. Still, it quickly became apparent that Benny wasn't taking the hint. "And?" Michael asked impatiently. "It was a black pickup, I think; I saw it pull into the lot just a few seconds before this guy walked in." Michael began circling his hand in front of Benny as a gesture to continue, "Make, model, year?" Benny shrugged his shoulders, "Now that I'm not exactly sure. I guess it was older, mid-eighties to early nineties, square body. Couldn't tell you a make. Normally, I can tell them apart, but I just wasn't paying attention to it so much that night..." Benny trailed off momentarily and then continued, "I never thought it would turn into this."

"Okay," Daniel said, annoyed, and let out a frustrated huff. "Anything else in particular about it?" "Well..." he started, "It was jacked up a few inches, nothing too showy, and had decent size mudders on it. Thirty-three's...thirty-five's maybe. But that ain't nothing special out here; that's eighty percent of the trucks out here in the country."

"Tell us about him," Detective Lugo said, intrigued, "anything you can." Benny looked up to the ceiling for a minute, gathering his thoughts. "White male, late twenties to early thirties. Average build, brown hair, and no beard, but not clean-shaven either. I guess a little more than a five o'clock shadow." Daniel was writing everything down as Benny was talking. "Okay, Benny, do you know what time they left?" Benny pondered his thoughts again, "Well, I think maybe a little after nine or something." Benny looked confused as he completed his sentence, "But they didn't leave together." Michael and Daniel snapped their heads together and then went back to Benny. "What do you mean they didn't leave together?" Michael asked persistently. "Well, she was at a table in the back; he came over from the bar." Benny pointed to the locations as he said, "They had several drinks together, but I guess he couldn't seal the deal. She got up and left; he stayed a bit longer before leaving himself." Daniel cut in before he could continue. "How much later did he leave?"

"Oh, I don't know, five minutes, ten at the most?"

"What did he do in that time before he walked out?"

"Just playing on his phone or some shit, I think." This time, Michael took over. "But you don't know for a fact that they didn't leave together, right?" Benny rocked his head from side to side, thinking, "Well, no, but..."

"But what?" Michael interjected angrily. "Did you actually see them leave the property separately?"

"Well... no... but he made some statement about striking out."

"Huh?" Michael and Daniel answered almost in unison. Daniel continued, "You spoke to him?" "She left... then he got up to leave too. As he passed the bar, he said something

about not picking her up, but I can't remember what it was...
I was just trying to clean up." Benny seemed incredibly
nervous as he recited this last statement. "I'm so sorry, if I
had known..."

"It's fine." Michael cut him off. "You didn't know;
there's no way you could have." Benny sighed in relief as if
he thought he might be taken in for not being of better
assistance. Michael was tapping his pen against his notepad,
"Is there anything else you can tell us about this guy?"
Benny shook his head, "I'm really sorry, offi... detectives. He
seemed decent enough, so I didn't pay him much attention."
"What about his receipt? Could we get a name from a
card?" Daniel asked persistently. Benny stared at him
expressionless momentarily, knowing they wouldn't like his
answer. He simply stated with a shaky voice, "Paid cash."
Daniel hung his head and squeezed his eyes shut in
annoyance. He really wanted to smack this man.

Michael and Daniel then gave the 'if you think of
anything' jargon and provided a business card. They finished
up their notes and left the bar. As they made it to the car,
they stopped and stared at each other across the top again.

"What do you think we should do now?" Michael asked.

"Let's push this shit out to the media right away," Daniel replied. Michael thought briefly, "You don't think it's too soon?"

"Fuck no. They already plastered that poor girl's name everywhere. Everyone already knows it happened. This is our first real lead. Get it out, get people talking, and who knows, maybe this will make our guy panic."

Chapter 11

It was now late afternoon on Tuesday, almost evening, and Edward was wrapping up his day at work. Edward had worked at the Atlantic Trading Company warehouse for the past few years. Mainly employed as a forklift operator, he was often tasked with other odd jobs around the floor. It was a simple job, but Edward liked it. He enjoyed the long days when multiple shipments were leaving the bay. It was an excuse for him to put in his headphones and zone out to his music for hours as he loaded the trucks to go. The company took care of its employees well. They never gave Edward a reason to leave, and he had no desire to do so anytime soon.

Edward had just finished his last loading project for the day. He sat and bullshitted with the truck driver before he set out on a five-day drive to deliver the products that were just loaded. Edward looked up at the sky as the truck took off from the bay. The sun started sinking into the horizon, and the temperature was cooling rapidly. The cool breeze let Edward know that autumn, his favorite season, was just around the corner. His eyes followed a flock of birds crossing the sky. They passed the tree line to where they couldn't be seen anymore, and Edward turned to head back in and gather his things.

Edward walked to his locker in the back room. He grabbed his phone, wallet, and keys and began stuffing them in all the correct pockets. Just to Edward's left was the entrance to the breakroom. It was closed off by a white door with a big glass window in the upper half. Through the glass, he saw several co-workers gathered in the corner where a small television sat. This intrigued his curiosity, so he decided to investigate the excitement.

As he walked in, he could pick up on multiple conversations happening. He looked at his co-worker, John, "What's going on?" John pointed to the television, "They just had a break in those murders. Said it's a white male driving an old black pickup truck." Panic began to shoot through Edward's body. *'Did someone see my truck? Was it on camera? Do they have my picture?'* An immediate nightmare appeared in his mind. Visions of the news placing a crude sketch on the screen while he stands right here, his co-workers immediately recognizing it as him and turning to him directly. To break his panic, Edward made a joke to John. "Well shit, I drive an old black pickup, it must be me." John chuckled and responded to him without taking his eyes off the television. "I mean fuck, it's Emerald. Half the population out here drives old pickups, many of which are black or dark."

This response began to ease Edward's concern. He began to think logically about it. As he watched the news segment, no pictures of him or his truck were shown,

meaning there were none. To the police and the rest of
Emerald, Edward was still a ghost. The whole segment was
the voiceover of an anchor while the camera panned around
an empty Benny's Tavern. But they did find out she was
there with someone, with him. Edward had already realized
that proactive steps needed to be taken from here; this
further solidified his belief. Edward said goodbye to John
and told him he had errands to run. Edward walked briskly
to the front entrance of the warehouse and then broke into
a swift jog to his truck. His anxiety was returning hastily.
Edward climbed into the truck and fired it up without
hesitation. He placed the truck in gear and vanished from
the property.

Anxiety was still permeating most of Edward's
evening. He skipped dinner and decided to take two
sleeping pills before crawling into bed just after 8:00 p.m. It
wasn't long before the drugs consumed his consciousness,
and Edward drifted into limbo.

As Edward drifted into a somber sleep, Benny Davenport was just heading home. He decided that after the events of the last few days, it was best to let one of his trusted employees close the bar tonight so he could turn in early. Benny needed to improve at taking time for himself. Often opening the bar at eleven in the morning, noon on Sundays, he would stay until the last call and then do some cleaning. Only three other employees were at the tavern; Only two he trusted to be there in his absence, and only one to trust enough to close the bar and empty the register into the safe.

Benny arrived at his apartment, dilapidated and dark; he walked towards the building with his hands in his pockets and eyes to the ground. He found his way to the stairs by navigating the cracks in the pavement the way a sailor would find his way through the stars. He had been making the same walk nightly for nearly twenty years now. It was not much, but Benny was never one for fruitful living. He had pondered moving to a nicer place from time to time. He could afford it as the bar did decent, but he would always fall on the logic that he spent more time at the bar and, therefore, should roll his money back into that.

He opened the door and walked inside, throwing his keys and wallet onto the table just inside the kitchen. He walked to the fridge and opened the door. Staring at almost nothing inside, he stood there for close to a minute, just feeling the cool air come over him. He shut it after retrieving nothing and plopped himself down on the couch.

As he sat on the couch across from his old box-style television, he stared into his own eyes in the reflection on the black screen. He didn't like the look of the man looking back at him. The man who didn't pay enough attention. The man who let an innocent woman fall to murder and who knows what else. *'Guess I struck out tonight.'* These words had been haunting him. *'Why did he say that to me? Why did he say that if he left with her? Did he catch her in the parking lot and change her mind? Did he force her in the truck?'* Benny knew it most likely was not force; someone would have seen or heard something if it had been. Too risky. *'Maybe he didn't want me knowing he left with her?'* Benny did not know the answer to his questions.

Benny lowered himself to the left side of his body to lie on the cushion. He didn't want to see the man on the screen anymore. He felt too exhausted to carry himself to bed. He pulled a couch pillow from the arm and slid it under his face. He closed his eyes and listened to the silence. A tear strolled down his nose and then dripped to his cheek. *'Guess I struck out tonight.'* Benny cried himself to sleep, only to be haunted by the nightmare of his own reality that Shannon had succumbed to. *'Guess I struck out tonight... Guess I struck out tonight... Guess I struck out tonight.'*

Chapter 12

Edward awoke to a frigid cold. His body was almost in shock, the pain of a thousand needles piercing his skin, encompassing his legs and torso. He quickly looked down at himself, once again staring at his naked body. No needles were impaling him; only snow and ice surrounded him. His body was almost entirely buried in the tundra. Edward sat himself up, bringing his legs in close for warmth. He could barely tell his body to move as it fought off the involuntary convulsions. As he breathed, his lungs seemed to fill with ice. He exhaled and watched the white cloud of hot breath travel several feet before dissipating into nothing.

Now, he stood and observed his surroundings. There was mainly snow, mountains, and pine trees, all covered in snow. Edward was on a slope. Most of the trees were up range from him, with a few stragglers placed sporadically. Down the hill was the edge of a cliff. It was only a hundred feet or so from his present location. However, the wind blurred his vision, picking up particles from the snow drifts surrounding him. The tiny ice particles carried on the wind pelted his face like miniature daggers.

He steadily made his way down the slope, stepping in shearing pain as his bare feet pierced through two feet of snow and ice with every step. As he walked, the wind howled from the trees behind him. He would surely die of hypothermia, Edward thought to himself. He made his way to the rocky cliff, placed one foot on the rock ledge to brace himself better, and peered over. The view below disappeared in the darkness. Although the moon was blazing, only the sun's intensity would be strong enough to reach the bottom beneath. Edward became afraid that the violent shaking of his body would cause him to tumble over the edge and plummet to his death.

He stepped back and turned around to the forest uphill from him. He caught a glimmer of something in the tree line for a split second. A dull green flicker of light vanished as quickly as
it appeared. Edward stood frozen again, his eyes scanning the tree line, looking for it again, but his sight failed him. He slowly began to move his feet up the hill. As he glanced back to the tree line, he caught another glimpse of light, yet this time red with an orangish-yellow hue. But it wasn't just one light; it was a pair. Edward maintained his footing towards the woods as his route options were limited.

Once again, a pair of lights appeared, followed by another, and then another. He quickly ascertained the source. *'Eyes.'* He thought to himself. But what did they belong to? Deer? Owls? He continued to creep up the hill when his questions were answered. A sudden howl echoed from the tree line, which set off a chain of others. *'Wolves'.* Edward didn't care to know how many, only to get away. He pivoted his bare, frigid feet in the snow and bolted in the other direction.

He began to run back down the slope. Still, he turned ninety degrees after suddenly remembering the unforgivable cliff ahead. He turned his head over his shoulder, watching the soft clouds of fresh powder form as his heels reared behind him. Although, through the clouds, he could see the eyes gaining on him, three pairs at least.

His lungs filled with an icy burn as he continued to sprint. He looked over his shoulder once again; this time, he could see the furry beasts behind him, snarling with teeth exposed as they closed in on him. He knew he wouldn't be able to outrun them. They drew closer and closer to him. Between the group, he could not determine if the sounds he heard were snarls or if they were close enough to snap at him.

He took a peek at the eyes with another glance behind him, a hundred feet at most. One broke from the group and went far to Edward's right. He knew exactly what was happening. Edward was being flanked by the wolves. *'Fuck! Fuck! Fuck!'* His immense panic grew to an unmeasurable size. His heart pounded deeply in his chest; he could almost hear it as he ran. Edward lengthened his stride to his maximum ability, but he could hear the closing distance from the beasts behind him.

As he ran out of gas, his legs slowed to a trot. His exhales exposed an exhausted and desperate plea. Tears flowed through the fear as his legs gave their final stride. He stopped and turned. The closest one leaped through the air once his body was bladed towards the animals. It seemed to soar at him in slow motion, its mouth opening to expose its razor-sharp teeth. Edward closed his eyes, waiting...

Chapter 13

Wednesday morning, just after eight thirty, Detective Bradley stands over his bathroom sink, his face covered in shaving cream. He turned the faucet hot and ran his blade under the water. He always felt the razor blades pull his whiskers less when it was hot, but he wasn't sure there was any science behind his theory to back it up. The television was on in the living room, and the news was busy notating the events of two nights prior on Randall Iverson's property. Michael tuned it out as he already knew the facts of the case and knew the station would, no doubt, be raping the truth with their own opinions or whatever other twisted fuck ideas they would insert to gain viewers. The police and the media always had a problematic relationship, both needing the other for something.

Michael dragged his razor down his face, watching the hair disappear from his skin and reappear, coating the porcelain sink as he rinsed the blade. His phone vibrated on the counter, echoing in the small bathroom. He looked down as he continued to shave. The preview of Detective Lugo's text displayed on the screen, "Where are you?'" Michael looked up at the corner of the screen to see the time. 8:37 a.m. The official report time in the office was 8:00 a.m., but Michael didn't care. He hadn't been late in years and knew there would be nothing more than a *"Don't be late again"* from his sergeant. He picked up his phone and replied, "Be there soon." He only got three drags on his razor before Detective Lugo sent another text stating, "Hurry." Michael knew it was important, but he just didn't have life today. This case was starting to drain both his physical and mental health. He didn't know how much longer he could spend his days in the office staring at a whiteboard, hoping for a lightbulb moment he knew would never come. He looked back down at his phone, *'this better be good,'* he thought.

It was just after nine before Detective Bradley rolled into the station parking lot. He exited his car, adjusted his tie, and threw his jacket over his shoulder. As he walked towards the building, he spotted a black Chevy sedan with U.S. Government tags. *'That's not a normal sight,'* Michael thought to himself. He walked through the lobby, past the elevator, to the stairwell. Michael has not been getting much exercise these days. He used to stay on top of his fitness, but it seemed to have subsided over time. It took an absolute plummet in the last two years. Walking up and down the stairs to his office daily appeared to be the extent of his cardio. The recent use of a new notch on his belt let him know it was time to get his shit back together.

Detective Bradley entered the office and saw a small gathering back by the cubbies where Detective Lugo and his desks sat. He immediately recognized two of the three men: Detective Lugo and their supervisor, Sergeant Lewis. As Michael walked up, the sergeant removed himself to head back to his office. He rendered a head nod in his direction. No statements about his late arrival have been made yet. The third gentleman was a younger white male in a stiff black suit and a black tie. The gentleman's waistline appeared as Michael rounded the corner of one of the cubbies. There, a tiny gold badge was peeking out from behind his coat. Michael didn't need to study it any further. That tiny little flash of gold and the government-issued vehicle in the parking lot was all Michael needed to put the puzzle together; it was the FBI. Michael let out a quiet and tired sigh as he approached the group to join in on a conversation that he already knew the subject of.

"This is Detective Bradley I was telling you about," Daniel said as he pointed, using the coffee mug still in his hand. "Just Michael," Detective Bradley responded as he lent his hand for a shake. "Michael," the man said as he returned the shake offer and continued, "I'm Agent Duffey with the Bureau, but Brad is fine as well."

Daniel stepped in, "Brad here says the Richmond office received a call from Lieutenant Ingram with the state police, stating we might need some assistance with this thing." The name sounded oddly familiar to Michael. He pondered it for just a second before it clicked. It was the Lieutenant from the Iverson farm two nights prior. *'That bastard,'* He thought to himself. *'Said he didn't want any part of our shit show and then made a back-channel call to the FBI to yank our case.'*

Michael looked back over to Brad, "Look... Agent Doofy," he stated sarcastically. "Duffey," He interrupted with slight annoyance. "Right," Michael said back condescendingly, "Agent Duffey, just like we told the Lieutenant with the state police two nights ago, we can handle this ourselves. I feel confident that most other agencies would not be any further than we are now." "I understand your frustration, Detective. I'm not here to take your glory." He paused and then continued. You and Detective Lugo will still be running this thing. I'm just here to offer some help and resources when needed. I don't need any credit."

"And what sort of resources would that be?" Michael inquired. "Well, our lab for one. We have our own in the field office; Much quicker turnaround than the state lab." "Well, everything that's been collected has already been sent to the state lab," Michael interjected. "Yes, I know," Brad stated as he turned to the desk behind him to retrieve a manila folder and continued. "We had them send the files over of anything they recovered; we got something." "Really?" Michael tried not to expose his excitement, but it proved quite tricky.

"It's not much, but it's a start." Agent Duffey opened the file and laid it on the desk in front of them. Inside were pictures of red and black flakes of something, but Michael could not tell what the flakes were from.

"Paint chips," Agent Duffey stated and further explained, "A low-quality urethane, the type used on vehicles. There were several flakes of it found in Shannon Reed's hair. Black on one side, red on the other." Daniel interjected himself into the conversation. "The bartender at

Benny's said our suspect was most likely driving a black or dark truck. If that's true, it shows that the truck he is driving used to be red, and the paint is starting to peel; it should make it a little easier to identify."

"Well, what if he was wrong?" Michael asked doubtfully. "That guy didn't seem too sure of anything. We could be looking for a red truck."

"Regardless, it's greatly narrowed down, and black is way more likely. We must go with that right now." Michael pondered this for a moment in silence before answering. "Alright, I'm sold for now. Did the lab get anything else?" This question was directed more to the new kid on the block. Agent Duffey recognized his cue. "Medical examiner should be done with the autopsy today. Still trying to determine the direct cause of death. She said there were two different ligature marks on Reed's neck. One was caused by the rope she was hanging from, but the M.E. says it's most likely post-mortem. She is still trying to identify what caused the other marks, but she stated there was also severe blunt force trauma to the back of her head."

"Alright," Michael said, impressed. "Guess we can start doing some canvassing for older trucks. I'll make some calls to local auto shops in town to see if anyone has done recent work on an older black truck with exposed red paint..." Michael sort of tapered off his statement as he walked to his desk. He wanted to waste no time. "That's great," Brad shouted in his direction as he continued walking. "Once our lab sends the request for the state Medical Examiner's office to go back over the first three girls, hopefully, we'll pick up something they missed." "Huh?" Michael stopped dead in his tracks and turned around, facing Brad and Daniel again. "The first three girls?" he asked in confusion. "Yeah, I want one of my people down there when they do a second autopsy on the victims, make sure they were thorough enough. I find it hard to swallow that nothing was found on the first go around with any of them. I wanna make sure it wasn't just a case of laziness or apathy."

Michael almost couldn't believe what he was hearing. "But those bodies were already released by the M.E.; they've all been buried," Michael said this, even though he knew this was already known information to everyone present. "Well, yeah..." Agent Duffey said, almost confused, as he looked at Detective Lugo. Daniel sort of hung his head; he already knew what was coming.

"Jesus fuck, man," Michael said disgustedly. He looked back and forth between Brad and Daniel, waiting for one of them to break the silence, but it did not come. "You're not seriously going to exhume those girls... to probably get nothing out of it."

"We don't know that," Brad said defensively. "Besides, I'll let the families get the final say. If they aren't on board, I won't back door it with a court order."

"I don't want there to be any false promises of hope for their cooperation," Michael asserted to Agent Duffey.

Brad raised his hands before him, "Hey, it will be legit. You guys can even make the calls if that makes you feel better." Michael shook his head and looked at Daniel, "Guess I'll start making some calls."

Chapter 14

Edward did not wake up until the afternoon on Wednesday. Just the usual chain of events after a night flooded with terrors. Edward lay in the bed with the blanket hanging halfway off his body. His core was hot but his skin was cool. Heavy sweating always accompanied his nightmares which would then seem to freeze on the surface of his skin, confusing his senses. This induced repetitions of kicking his blanket off his body only to pull it back on moments later.

He pulled the covers from his body, enjoying the rush of cold air that struck his skin. He quickly got up and stumbled into the shower. He rubbed his eyes vigorously as the steamy water cascaded over him. He only remained in there for a moment before stepping out. He wrapped his waist in a towel and used his hand to wipe the condensation off the mirror. He looked at himself, observing his two-day beard blending into his slightly thinning hair. He ran his fingers atop of his head, wondering how many years he had until he would have to choose between a shaved head or the hideous horseshoe that desperate men hang onto. *'Five? Ten? Maybe fifteen years? If I should be so lucky.'*

Edward pulled an old T-shirt over his head. He didn't know if it was clean, and he didn't care. Edward had the midnight shift tonight at the warehouse, and he knew he should still be sleeping for a few more hours, but he couldn't. He didn't know how much more abuse his body could take working alternating shifts: day shift this day, midnight shift that day, evening shift another day. Being at the bottom of the employee totem pole had its disadvantages for shift preference. Edward had always struggled to keep the same job for more than a year at a time, often let go from too many callouts due to poor sleep... or poor work performance due to, you guessed it... poor sleep. It was a curse to more than just waking up tired and fear of the night.

Edward had to run errands in town. He figured he might as well get up and do them now instead of trying to obtain sleep he knew would never come. If lucky, he could come back after and get a few-hour nap in before work. Doubtful, but Edward wanted to stay optimistic about the situation. Edward collected his keys, wallet, and phone and left the house to head into town.

Chapter 15

"Thank you again, ma'am. You have no idea how much this might help us," Michael said genuinely. "I understand, Detective, anything to help find the demon that did this to my baby girl." Detective Bradley sighed heavily into the phone and stared at the keyboard on his desk. "I'll let you know the minute we find something; you and your husband will be the first to hear."
"Thank you again."

Detective Bradley hung up the phone as Detective Lugo walked up behind him. "So? How did it go?"
"Hannah Vermond's parents are in; the others basically told me to fuck off." Michael huffed and then continued. "They don't think it will help us out anymore and don't want their bodies desecrated."
"Hey, one is better than none." Daniel sounded less than optimistic in his response. Doubt was starting to spread in the department after Shannon's death, and the increased concern and judgment from the community were not

relieving any of the pressure. Michael looked up from his desk across the bullpen to Brad Duffey, who worked at a makeshift workspace beside the wall heater. Michael nodded his head in Duffey's direction, "We'll let our fed friend do the paperwork on the exhumation; it was his idea anyway."

"I'll let him know they're on board." Daniel walked away and headed to Brad. Michael remained slouched in his chair, pondering the events to come. He prayed it would pay off in the long run, but nobody could be certain.

Chapter 16

It was almost three in the afternoon. Edward had completed most of his errands, picking up a few groceries and a trip to the bank. The weather seemed perfect to him, a cool, crisp air with the aroma of autumn lingering in his senses. A light jacket with rolled-down windows made for the ideal car ride through town and country. Edward turned right onto South Main Street and listened to the engine rumble under the hood of his truck. The truck was beaten up these days, both cosmetically and mechanically, but Edward didn't care too much. He would continue to fix it until it wasn't worth it anymore; perhaps it had already reached that point, and he was just in denial.

Edward continued to drive down the strip when something caught his eye. It was not so much a *'something'* that captured his gaze but rather a *'some-one.'* That someone was a beautiful young lady, maybe mid-twenties. She was blonde with her hair in a ponytail, wearing leggings with a light hoodie, and toting a small duffle bag, most likely coming from the gym just up the block. She was walking the opposite way that Edward was driving on South Main. He then passed her and took over his observations by following her in his sideview mirror and then his rearview mirror as the distance grew. She then turned the corner, and she was gone.

Edward pulled his truck over to the side of the road but left it running. Edward felt one of his urges emerging, both inside of his mind and inside of his pants. Edward's sleep has been suffering intensely lately. He knew there would be no time to play if he wanted any chance of sleep before work that night. He put the truck back in gear and then began to pull off from the sidewalk but quickly hit the brake pedal and stopped just a few feet from the curb. He could not just let it go. He could not let *her* go.

He made a quick U-turn in the roadway and went back to the intersection of South Main and Conway. He looked right and saw the woman still walking down the right side of the road. Edward kept his distance, afraid she would pick up on his loud engine rumbling. He followed her for a few more turns, heading towards the edge of town until she made her final turn on Hamilton Avenue. The woman stopped and checked the mailbox stand just outside one of the apartment buildings on the block. *'Must be home,'* Edward said to himself in his head. He pulled the truck over once again and quickly turned the engine off. This caught her attention as she quickly glanced in his direction but did not look at anything. She seemed to fumble through a stack of mail and then shoved it into the front pocket of her hoodie. She then entered the building.

It was only a three-story apartment building and appeared to have an apartment on either side of the stairwell at each level. A window on the front of the building exposed the stairwell. Edward's eyes followed her up the stairs to the third floor and into the apartment on the right. She went in and was gone. Edward looked up and down the street but did not see much foot traffic. He sat there momentarily, deciding if this was the proper time and place to do this. *'Maybe I can come back tonight.'* Edward thought about it for a minute, but the erection in his pants would not let him leave. His urge was too strong to go home now. Even if he did leave, he knew his urge would only fester both in his body and in his mind. It would most likely cause him to masturbate in the bathroom and, in turn, kill his urge for the night. Edward knew that was the better, safer alternative. Still, it was not the course of action he desperately desired.

Edward got out of his truck and began to walk towards the building. He made it to the door and stood there for a moment. He looked at the call box hanging next to the door. An old stainless-steel block with a green screen and keypad. His eyes wandered to a list of names below. There were two apartments on each floor, one on each side

of the stairwell, labeled Apartments A and B. His vision slid
down to the third floor, assuming apartment B was on the
right. The line read "Victoria Walmsley"- seemed fitting
enough. He read apartment A to be sure; "Edwin Caldwell."

'Bingo,' he said to himself. Edward wet his lips and
mouthed the word "Victoria." He could already imagine
himself sliding inside of her... finishing inside of her. Edward
took a deep breath and composed himself. He stuck his right
hand out and grasped the metal handle of the glass door. He
gave it a soft pull, and it opened gently. Edward began to
walk inside and made it to the stairwell just a few feet
inside. Once his foot hit the first stair, he could hear
someone else coming down. As he began to round the first
corner, he was met by a young black female heading down
to leave. Exceptionally beautiful and innocent looking, she
let out the softest "excuse me" as she turned sideways and
squeezed by in the narrow landing. She continued down
without looking back, but there was no denying she smiled
at him through her eyes when they met. Edward stood on
the landing and watched her exit to the street. So young and
smooth-looking. Edward closed his eyes, suddenly
aroused. 'No,' he told himself. 'I'm not here for her.'

Edward continued up the stairs to the third floor. He stopped on the landing and stared at the door. The excitement was mounting inside of him. He took another few breaths to calm it. *'Excitement leads to mistakes.'* He pressed his left ear to the door. He could hear movement inside, but nothing erratic. Edward placed his right hand on the doorknob to test if it was unlocked. He turned it gently, and it gave way, proving unlocked.

The next part could be quite cumbersome: opening the door and going inside unheard. Edward used his unique trick. Doors were often loose in the door jamb and frame. Sometimes, opening the door slowly can make the door rattle and bring unwanted attention. Edward discovered long ago to pull the door tight against the frame. Then, he uses his other hand to press against it to create pressure. This kept the door tight between his hands and prevented rattling if he could hold his hands steady. He turned the knob again. He began to maneuver the door open slightly, only enough to peer inside. It seemed to open towards the kitchen; nothing else could be seen. Edward quickly slipped inside and shut the door delicately. He stood there, adrenaline pumping through him. For a moment, the only noise he could hear was his heart beating itself out of his chest. He pulled his bowie knife out of the sheathing. He could hear movement from a room in the back. Edward could identify the noise as a dresser drawer opening and closing. He moved to the hallway and stood there, lying in wait.

It was only a few moments before Victoria exited from the bedroom. She turned from the door down the hall, looking down at her phone before the shadow in her peripheral vision alerted her to the intruder. She looked up and turned to stone. Her body was still, but her eyes were frantic. Looking upon a dark figure before her, her mouth began to utter something but was immediately cut off.

"Don't scream," Edward said in a low, soft, yet assertive voice. "I'm sorry I have to do this." Edward charged at her. Victoria let the phone fall from her hand, so instilled with fear, she forgot it existed there. She turned around to run; however, as she turned away from Edward, he caught her ponytail with his left hand, instantly wrapping it around his fist. He simultaneously brought his blade across the front of her neck with his right hand. He pulled it across hard and deep, feeling the resistance of her flesh. Blood instantly spewed from the opening. An initial burst freckling the walls, then quickly began pouring down the front of her body. She fell to her knees but was yanked onto her back by Edward as he propelled his fist, still grasping her hair to the floor.

Victoria grabbed her neck, attempting to stop the bleeding. She knew she was failing and began to shake from fear and shock. Edward walked around her and straddled her legs as he got down on his knees. Victoria attempted to speak, proving near impossible, "Please..." She whispered and paused. "Baby... I'm pregnant." Edward looked down at her, initially thinking she was calling him baby, but then realized she was referring to one growing inside her with the latter statement.

Edward looked at her dying eyes and then trailed down her dirty body to her stomach. A disgusted look emerged on his face. *'What a whore,'* He thought to himself as he looked down on her, displeased. Edward knew he needed to take care of her immediately. He lifted his knife above his head and then forcefully plunged it into her stomach. Edward felt the knife harpoon straight into her body. He was always intrigued by its sound as it penetrated the body cavity. Victoria's body lurched upwards, causing a burst of blood to spew out of her, once again freckling the walls and the carpet around her body. Victoria's head fell back to the ground. She was dead.

Edward looked over her, admiring what he was doing. The entire front of her body was painted in her own blood. *'I might have to clean her up a little before I play.'* Edward knew there was an immense chance he would end up covered in blood as well, and being spotted before returning to the truck would prove to be quite dire for him. He momentarily pondered the thought just before another idea was born into his mind. Edward rolled her over and examined the body. There was much less blood on the backside of her. Edward looked down at her supple buttocks in those tight leggings. *'Oh, Victoria, why do you taunt me with such a good time?'*

Suddenly, a cry was heard. Edward's head and eyes shot up, and they stared down the hall. At first, he asked himself what it was, but he knew all too well. It was the cry of an infant. *'Baby...pregnant.'* Victoria uttered the words just before she died. She was not saying, "Baby, pregnant." Was she saying, *"I have a baby, and I'm pregnant?"* Edward quickly stood up from his knees and glared down the hall.

His feet began to carry him forward, carefully sidestepping the body and the blood that was already seeming to harden on the carpet fibers. As he made his way closer to the back bedroom, he heard further rustling and the outcries of an infant. He entered the room slowly and observed a nursery. Painted in white and grey, covered in elephant décor. He saw the crib in the corner. A blanket was hanging over the railing, concealing what was behind it. As he approached, a young face emerged in front of him. It was a baby but not quite the infant stage. It was a boy, appearing to be maybe ten months old, perhaps a year. *'How is she pregnant again already?'* He shook the thought off immediately; it was a moot point now. The boy smiled at him and reached his tiny hand up to him. Edward stared at the boy in contempt. *'What to do with him now?'*

'The girl!' A wave of panic washed over Edward immediately. The girl he had passed in the stairwell just inside the entrance. She was leaving just after Victoria had arrived. There was no one else in here with the baby besides Victoria. Victoria did not have the child as she entered the building. The girl was babysitting the baby. There did not seem to be any other viable option. Once this is out, she can describe me to the police. *'She saw my face!'* Edward screamed in his head. *'Breathe...breathe...breathe.'* Edward took slow breaths through his nose and let them exit slowly out of his mouth. 'It's *ok, everything will be fine.'*

Edward gathered himself. Problems had certainly arisen; there was no doubt about that: a baby and a witness. *'How could I be so careless?"* Edward began to question if his desires and urges had begun to cloud his judgment. If so, errors could have been made on previous kills. But there was no time to waste thinking of that now. The witness would have to be dealt with later, but as for now, there were more pressing issues. First, the child. Second, Edward's prize was still lying out in the hallway.

He looked down at the child, a young boy holding some sort of a ring toy in his hand. Edward was not sure if this was a teething toy or something else. It didn't matter. He reached down and rubbed the boy's head, leaving a small stamp of his mother's blood on his scalp. Edward knew the child would be a significant distraction during his time with Victoria. "This is my time now, child."

Edward walked back to the hallway where Victoria lay. He circled around the body until he stood in the very place where he had unsheathed his knife and placed it inside of her. He leaned over, grasped the handle, and ripped it out of her stomach. A small strand of liquid blood ran down the edge of the blade onto the floor. He stood over her for a minute, admiring her and envisioning what was yet to come with her.

A moment later, he was back in the bedroom with the child. Edward knew what he had to do. He had never done this before, not to a child. Although adverse feelings of killing had never run through him before, something was birthed in him. It wasn't fear nor doubt; He knew it must be done. Edward shook his head and his mind to clear his thoughts. His feelings were not of importance right now. His eyes drifted to the foot of the crib where a crochet pillow lay. A soft green with white embroidered lettering on the front that read "mommy's boy" in all lowercase. He picked it up, once again leaving another trace of Victoria's blood. He stuffed the pillow and knife under his right arm and gently guided the child to lie down with his left hand while making his best effort to "shush" him. Edward couldn't remember a time he had shushed a child before, and to say it came out naturally could not have been further from the truth.

Once the child was down, it began to fuss. Edward knew he needed to get this over with. He then pulled the pillow from under his arm and placed it across the child's face and body. Just a second later, he raised his knife in a similar fashion to what he had done to the boy's mother and brought it back down through the pillow with great force. There was a single jerk and nothing more, not a peep or cry. Edward let go and saw the knife standing up in the pillow. A small pool of red was now forming in the crib. Edward looked down at the still pillow in the crib. He didn't want to see what was beneath it. This was not part of his plan and was undoubtedly an unwelcome intrusion. He pulled the knife back out through the pillow effortlessly. He turned and exited the bedroom. He never set foot in it again.

Edward returned to Victoria in the hallway and looked over her body again. He was finally ready. He began undressing her in a delicate way. He placed the blood-soaked clothing adjacent to her body in a pile out of his way. She was now on her back, naked. Edward pulled out his headphones and turned on his music, playing lightly in his ears. '*Soft cello.*' He then ran his face down the front of her body, just barely hovering above her skin. He could feel the static tension between his skin and hers. He stopped just above her clitoris. He gently spread her legs and pressed his face in between. Her skin was freshly shaved, so soft and smooth. An erection formed immediately. Edward took in a long, slow inhale through his nostrils to smell her. She smelled so fresh, even after coming from the gym. He took another breath. It was so invigorating that it overwhelmed his other senses. He placed his left cheek against her groin again, enjoying the softness of her skin once more. He didn't want to let up from it.

After a moment, Edward spread her legs to expose her more. He placed his face down again to her. He let out a hot breath and then stuck his tongue out and dragged it across her labia from the bottom, sliding up to the top. He enclosed his mouth around her clitoris and sucked on it. Edward then pulled her legs in close, pressing her thighs against his cheeks. Still warm, he could only imagine how much she would have enjoyed this. He pulled his lips away, just grazing her clitoris with his teeth as he let go. He looked up at her sweet face. "How was that darling?" He said softly, almost whispering to her. He continued to rub her clitoris as he looked upon her. "Yeah, I know," Edward smiled to himself, amused with himself, impressed with himself for his oral performance.

Just as he had done with Shannon, he pulled his face in close to hers. He grabbed her petite chin with his left hand and tilted her head to her right, exposing her left cheek to him. He stuck his tongue out and laid it flat on her cheek at the jawline and dragged it up her face slowly. He loved the taste of her skin. His tongue was tickled by the tiny peach fuzz that covered her face. He repeated the act several more times. With each repetition, he slid his tongue slower and slower to take her in. He finished, shoved his face into her hair, and inhaled until his lungs could take in no more. The smell intoxicated him. He slid his nose back and forth along her scalp through the thick hair. He wanted to live inside that smell, but Edward had other tasks to complete.

Edward reached into his pocket and pulled out a condom. He unzipped and placed it over his erect penis. By this time, he was throbbing so hard he knew he would cum almost immediately after entering her. 'I've *had enough fun with the front.'* Edward rolled her over and couldn't help but stroke himself as he looked at her. Her beautiful brown hair draped down the back of her shoulders, her back, her buttocks so supple. He reached out and ran his hand from her right shoulder down her back. He slid his hand onto her right butt cheek and squeezed it. How could something be so soft and firm at the same time? His hand held the base of her cheek, and he continued to squeeze and then spread her open, exposing her anus to him. Edward let go of her with his hand.

He lowered himself down between her legs, placing his stomach on the plush carpet. He then pressed his face firmly between her buttocks. He lay there for a moment, his face completely buried in her flesh. Edward once again took in a slow but forceful inhalation through his nose. His nostrils flared, taking in her scent. What a sweet aroma. Her own brand of fragrance was so invigorating, but Edward refused to be tantalized by something he could not take. He would get his taste.

Edward reached up with both hands and placed them on each perspective side of her buttocks. He once again spread her open and exposed her anus. This was followed by placing his tongue on her. The flat surface of it grazed over her anus and then rimmed the opening with the tip of his tongue. He continued to do this for a moment before finally penetrating her anus with his tongue. Her taste overwhelmed him. Edward stopped before he over-aroused himself with her, ruining his grand finale.

Edward pulled his pants down close to his knees. He grabbed the base of the condom and entered her from behind. The lubricant on the condom certainly helped enter such a tight space, but an ample amount of force was still required. Once inside, it was apparent that this would be a short endeavor. Edward thrust himself in her several times before approaching his climax. He thrust as hard and fast as he could until he felt the acute eruption begin to take place. The moment was so intense that his body froze as it happened. As his body convulsed, he could feel himself filling the condom up quickly. Once done, he looked down at her from behind. *'Fuck, you're good."* Edward secured the base of the condom again as he slid out. He looked down on her again, admiring his work, but much work still needed to be done.

He stepped over her body and went down the hall to the bathroom on the left, directly across the hall from the child's room. He went in and began to run a bath. He sat on the edge of the tub. He watched the water hit the base and circle the drain before flowing down, intermittently reaching out to test the temperature. Once it was right, he pushed the drain stop down to let the water build up. Edward walked back to the hallway, making a direct effort not to avert his attention to what was in the room across from him. Once he was over Victoria, just like the others, he bent over and grabbed her by the hair. He dragged her to the bath, leaving a sinister trail of blood on the soft white carpet.

Once in the bathroom, he lifted her over the edge of the tub and dumped her in. She hit the water with a flat thud. A wave of water spilled over the ledge onto the floor. The water settled, and she lay there half floating, half sunk in the tub. Edward looked up at the shower rack and scanned the abundance of shampoo and conditioner bottles. Not knowing what the hell he was looking at, he snatched one at random. He flicked the lid open with his thumb and began dumping it over her. Holding the bottle at his shoulder level, he drizzled it over her in a zig-zag pattern from head to toe until her entire body was covered. He closed the bottle and threw it back on the shelf.

Edward knelt down beside her, causing the jean fabric over his knees to soak in the water from the tile floor. 'Fuck.' He looked up at her disgusting body, annoyed, pulled his sleeves up to his elbow, and began to dunk her dirty body in the water over and over, attempting to agitate it and activate the soap. The process was repeated until it seemed to do the job. Edward reached in, released the drain plug, and watched the water lever subside rapidly around her.

Once empty, he turned the water back on but pulled the stop to send the water to the shower head. He removed the shower head from above and washed her down, using it as a hose until she was clean. Once he felt the wash was complete, he hung the shower head back onto its hook.

Edward walked out of the bathroom and went to the kitchen. He grabbed a paper towel, wrapped it around his hand as a makeshift glove, and began to search the drawers for a pad and pen; success was on the second pull. He walked over to the tiny breakfast nook table and sat down as he wrote a passage out. This was a good one indeed. He then walked into the bathroom and used the paper towel to wipe down anything he may have touched. Edward finished up the job and walked towards the front door of the apartment. He turned around and took one last look. *'My God, it's a mess in here.'* The door closed behind him. The room was left in a soft, quiet chaos.

Chapter 17

Edward woke up just after one in the afternoon on Thursday. He had gone to work just a few hours after finishing with Victoria. He entered as his calm, usual self. His regular routine ensued of taking a piss, grabbing a cup of coffee in the break room, and then hopping on his forklift. Edward went from eleven to seven in the morning, moving pallets of product from the storage shelves to the shipping bay where the morning shift would immediately begin loading them onto the incoming trucks lined up in the parking lot at clock-in time. Although they would be busy, Edward had enjoyed his slow, quiet night.

Edward hadn't made it home, was not in bed until almost eight in the morning, and didn't drift into dreamland until nearly nine. These few hours appeared to be all he would be getting for the day. It didn't matter anyway; he knew his sleep would be a short batch today. In just a bit, he had another scheduled session with Dr. Brown. Kenny Brown had been his therapist for six months, Just another one in a lineup of many. Although Edward had been in therapy since sixteen, one never seemed to last more than a year or so. The parting of each one was usually followed by a six-to-nine-month hiatus before finding another one.

Edward knew he needed help with his mind. He knew he was sick, but... could he even be cured? He usually parted after he got too close to them and opened up too much. He didn't want them to know *too* much. Edward really liked Dr. Brown, though. He wasn't exactly honest with the doctor about everything, leaving out the obvious. Edward knew there were certain disqualifiers to doctor-patient confidentiality, and he did not feel comfortable testing those waters.

Deep inside, Edward knew his mind couldn't be fixed without being honest with his doctor, but honesty would cost him his freedom. But what is freedom? Freedom in life and freedom of the mind can be opposites, and obtaining one could mean abstaining from the other. Edward proceeded to get dressed, eat a bowl of stale cereal, and then drive into town to meet with his doctor.

Edward arrived just a few minutes before the session was to begin. His truck swung into the closest spot out front, and he let the engine idle as he looked to the autumn sky. The cool breeze wafted through the open window. John Anderson sang on the scratchy radio channel that barely came in from Richmond. The static and distortion of the interference reminded Edward of an old record that had been played too many times for loving ears. Edward gathered himself and went inside.

Upon entry to the office, he did the usual process of signing in, taking a seat, and flipping through two-year-old magazines that he was never actually reading. Today, the choice was Classic Muscle Cars of America. Edward didn't know much about cars besides the standard oil, tire change, and other minor repairs. Still, he enjoyed looking at them and admiring their beauty. A good body on a car was almost as sexy as a good body on a woman.

The office phone rang; the receptionist picked it up and simply stated, "Okay, I'll send him back." She looked at Edward and said, "Edward, he's ready for you."
"Thanks." He stood up from his chair and went through a large wooden door leading to a small office hallway. There were two doors on the right, and Edward went in. "Good

afternoon," Edward stated tiredly. Edward, how good to see you; how have you been?"

"Eh, I'm alive." He replied poutingly as he reached the sofa across from Dr. Brown. Edward sat directly in the center, causing him to sink in between the two cushions. Edward thought it might be time for an upgrade; Lord knows the doctor could afford it with what he charges. Edward had always sat on the sofa. Television and movies always depicted the poor saps in these offices lying face up to the ceiling while crying about God knows what. However, Edward always felt silly at the thought of lying down while talking to someone. He was also hesitant that if he had, the doc would hit him with a *'you know, people don't really do that.'* Edward guessed some mysteries are better off staying unsolved.

"I missed you at our last appointment. I was hoping everything was okay. Are you sleeping alright?" Edward smirked at the question and briefly raised an eyebrow. "I'm getting a few hours a night, or day at least."

"You've been taking the pills? Are they helping?"

"They help, better than nothin', I suppose. Maybe I need something stronger, or maybe just something different. Can you do that for me?"

"Well, Edward, I told you before I'm an L.P.C, I can't prescribe you anything. But if you're still under the care of Dr. Ball, I can email him and see if he's willing to try something different for you."

Dr. Ball was Edward's Psychiatrist. That was another thing Edward always felt the movies got wrong; on the silver screen, it was the psychiatrist the saps laid down for on the couch. Still, when Edward was referred to Dr. Ball, it seemed he would pop in for a five-minute conversation, write a script for something, and be advised to seek counseling from a psychologist or a licensed professional counselor.

"Yeah, that'd be great," Edward replied in his best Bill Lumbergh impression. The joke didn't seem to stick. *'Must have a shit taste in movies.'* "Well..." Doc Brown didn't look up while writing a note, "I'll send him an email after our session; how's that?" He finally looked up with a scrunched expression, seemingly attempting to prevent his glasses from sliding off his greasy nose. "Sure. Sounds great."

"Great."

Doc continued the conversation, "So, Edward. Where do you wanna pick up this week? It seems your biggest issue right now is sleep or the lack thereof. How have the nightmares been this past week?"

"Umm... two, I think. Pretty intense ones, enough to keep me from going back to sleep after I have them." Edward lifted his palms off his thighs, giving a *'well, there's that'* gesture if such a thing existed.

"Uh-huh-uh-huh, have you been trying the sleep exercises I gave you? Are they helping?"

"Oh... you know, I really gave them a shot for a bit, but they just didn't seem to do the trick. I don't know; maybe I wasn't doing them quite right, but I think I was." That was a lie. Edward tried the exercises once and thought it was just about the dumbest shit he had ever heard. The doc had provided him with a C.D. of some jackass voicing over calming noises telling him to squeeze and let go of his hands, his feet, his mind, or what have you. If Edward had honestly guessed how long he lasted, it would have been under two minutes. "Oh, that's okay. They're certainly not for everyone, but the more you practice, the better it seems to work. You just hang on to that disc if you want to give it another try."

"Sure thing, doc."

"Now Edward, last time we left off... I know you don't like to talk about it... that night when your mother was taken. I know you said you don't remember much, but I really feel that if we can dive deep into that... I don't necessarily want you to re-live it. Still, I think if you can come to terms with that night, the events, that we can really make some progress with your trauma that I believe is the root of your nightmares and sleeping issues."

"I really don't remember much, honestly. It was so long ago. It seems like the more I try to remember, the foggier it gets."

"Uh-huh, uh-huh. Edward, let me ask you something. What do you know about hypnotherapy?"

"Hypnosis?" Edward let out a chuckle. "Like, put me under a spell and retrieve my memories?"

The doc let out a hefty chuckle as well. "Well, no, not exactly," Dr. Brown continued. "I have a friend of mine, a close friend that I trust dearly. We went to graduate school together. He has done extensive research in this field and has been practicing it for some years now. Of course, it's not applicable in every therapy path, but in your case, I really think it would help us see what hasn't been seen since that night." Edward thought about it for a minute. "I don't know, man, that seems kinda showy. Is there any proof that it works?" The doc pondered his thoughts for a moment before responding. "Well, I think there's an abundance of research that would support that the results are quite accurate to the incidents that occurred. Of course, there has been speculation that with suggestable clients that, maybe certain memories were introduced to the client by the proctor rather than retrieved from actual memories." Doctor Brown took a minute to clear his throat before continuing. "Of course, the recipe for that would be a mixture of a rather suggestible patient and a proctor not particularly well versed in the practice, or even one that might engage in an inappropriate attempt to introduce a falsehood to what was there. Now, it would be a low probability, in general, for that to happen, and I don't sense you to be the suggestible type. I would never dare expose a patient of mine to any exercise conducted by someone less than professional, or that would act in such malpractice."

Edward seemed impressed with what the doc laid out to him. He felt silly engaging in these sorts of acts, but he'd be lying if he said he wasn't intrigued. "Alright, doctor, if you think it could work, I'd be willing to give it a try."

"Wonderful, I'll reach out to him and see if we can make it work for your next appointment. I'll let you know ahead of time if it doesn't, and we can reschedule for another time. Of course, I will have to disclose some of the discussions we've had so he has a decent base of information on what to look for. I would need your permission to do so before we could move forward. Is that okay?"
"Yeah, sure."

Edward remained on the sofa for another twenty minutes, talking with Doctor Brown to finish his meeting. The doctor covered a few different sleep exercises he felt that Edward might feel more comfortable with and emailed

Dr. Ball while he was still in the office. They shook hands and parted ways. Not much was covered in the session today, but Edward could not deny his curiosity of what may be revealed, of what was shut out.

Chapter 18

Shortly after Edward was heading home from his afternoon visit with Doctor Brown, Detective Bradley, and Detective Lugo were wrapping up their day at work. Not much was accomplished that day, once again spent reviewing the same list of bullshit leads that lead to nowhere. The local news stations had all started advertising that anyone with information should call the Emerald Police Department. Unfortunately, this led to dozens of tips that, off face value alone, seemed ridiculous. The follow-ups that ensued only reassured these judgments. To both detectives, it felt they had made a hundred calls between them over the last two days, with no information gathered worthy of following up with.

Detective Bradley checked his email one last time before closing out his computer and heading home. While mindlessly reading a generic county email that served no real purpose to him, he heard the main doors leading into the bullpen open, followed by rapid footsteps. Michael looked over his left shoulder to see the FBI's gift to Emerald, Agent Duffey, approaching the cubicles. Michael turned back to his computer quickly and huffed out an agitated sigh. *'I don't have the energy for this shit right now.'*

"Gentleman." Agent Duffey boasted as if giving a proclamation. "Hello, Special Agent," Michael miffed in his most exaggerated tone. "What can we do for the federal government?"

"How about what I can do for you? Or what did I do for you?" Michael had to admit he was intrigued now. He spun around in his swivel chair to face Agent Duffey. "How's that?" At this point, Detective Lugo came about from his cubicle and simply addressed Brad with a nod. This simple act of acknowledgment was significantly preferred to Michael's sarcasm.

"The autopsy is finished on Miss Reed, Shannon. Turns out the paint chips weren't the only piece of evidence that was left behind." Brad had both detectives' attention now. "Well?" Detective Lugo questioned impatiently. Agent Duffey opened the folder he was holding, pulled out a large, printed photo, and placed it on the table beside him. He slid it over for Michael and Daniel to look at. It appeared to be some sort of red fiber. The picture seemed to be a massively blown-up view to show the fibers more clearly.

"Red fibers?" Michael asked. Agent Duffey responded, "Carpet fibers, to be exact, and 80-20 loop carpet, to be even more specific."

"80-20 carpet?" Michael asked, "Am I supposed to know what that means?"

"Automotive carpet," Detective Lugo responded immediately. Michael thought to himself, of course, the hobbyist mechanic would know that.

"That's right," Agent Duffy said with a smirk before continuing, "Automotive carpet, nylon. Most prominently used from the late seventies to the mid-nineties. These fibers were found embedded in the rope that was used to hang her from the tree."

"He kept the rope in his truck, probably under the seat," Michael thought out loud.

"Bingo."

"Okay..." Daniel began a thought and paused as he gathered it. "Okay, so now we know the truck's interior is red; the truck itself is most likely black, possibly red." Michael continued Daniel's facts, "And the use of the carpet fits the general frame of model that Benny said the truck was: late eighties to early nineties."

"Any chance we can narrow down a make of vehicle that used this type of carpet in their cars during these years?" Michael asked Agent Duffey, almost expecting Daniel to answer his question again.

"Eh... not particularly, most likely a domestic. I think we can count imports out for now, perhaps focusing on the big American brands during that time. I can always do a little research to see if there's any evidence to support that.

"I know it doesn't seem like much, but I think this could really start putting us in the right direction. Do you guys want me to push this out to the media at all?"

"No," Michael responded immediately. "Let's hold this to ourselves." Daniel agreed with him, "Yeah, second that. His vehicle info is already out there; he knows it. There's no way this asshole isn't watching the news or seeing something about it online. He may ditch the truck or alter it if we get too specific. This can really narrow down the pool of trucks we're looking for. Let's not screw it up."

Michael chimed back in towards Agent Duffey, "When is the exhumation taking place for Hanna Vermond?" "We're moving fast on it," Agent Duffey assured assertively. "The exhumation is taking place tomorrow at noon sharp. I'll be there for you all to make sure it goes smoothly. The body will be sent directly to the field office in Richmond. The medical examiner will start going over her again first thing Monday." Michael started to think maybe Agent Duffey wasn't too bad. He quickly shot his own thought down, *'Nah, still too much of a boy scout for me.'*

"Anything else discovered in the autopsy with Shannon? Other than the fibers?" Daniel asked, still looking at the photo. "Well, nothing else was pulled off the body, but as you may recall, they originally mentioned there were two types of ligature marks on the neck. One believed to be postmortem, the rope obviously. The other, they believe, was most likely a belt, approximately one and a half inches wide; not much to tell on it other than that. This was most likely what he used to strangle her. Unless we find a suspect very soon, the likelihood of locating that belt is slim. The odds of finding any DNA on it at this point are basically none."

Michael pursed his lips with a tilted eyebrow and slightly nodded his head in acknowledgment as he pondered this in his mind. "Well, we have something to start. With any luck, something will turn up with Hannah that we can link to Shannon. But let's not get too optimistic; let's wait and see what turns up." Michael paused momentarily to see if anyone had anything else to contribute to the conversation. When it was apparent that they did not, he got back into the mood of going home. "Well, boys, I think that does it for the day. Agent Duffey, I appreciate the help and the info. Let us know how the exhumation goes tomorrow; we will both still be knocking out these leads so we can cross them off." "No trouble at all." The men proceeded to grab their things and headed home.

Several hours later that night, Michael got ready for bed, climbed on top of the mattress, and pulled the comforter over himself. As he lay there, staring at the ceiling, he pondered the information that had been revealed. For once, Michael felt optimistic about the case. A glimmer of hope, a genuine lead. A wave of relief and calmness came over him as he closed his eyes. He was finally relaxed and knew he could get some solid rest tonight. Michael drifted off, not knowing this would be the last night he would sleep for weeks to come.

Chapter 19

Friday morning, just before noon, FBI Special Agent Duffey was pulling into Summerset Memorial Park in preparation for the exhumation of Hannah Vermond. He swung his black, government-issued sedan into one of many open spots outside a small office building just inside the main gate. As he shut his car off, a middle-aged man- a quite portly fellow- exited the building. The man was dressed in dirty overalls and had a short but fat cigar hanging out of his mouth. The man took a puff, staring at Brad Duffey, presumably waiting for him to approach him.

Agent Duffey threw the man a wave as he greeted him, "Good morning, how are you doing today, Sir?" "Heya, you the man from the gov'ment? For the diggin'?" Agent Duffey was slightly put off by the teeth that showed through the man's mouth as he spoke. An accurate model of what poor dental hygiene was. "Uh, well, I'm Special Agent Duffey with the FB....." "You got the papers?" the man interrupted. *'Papers?'* Agent Duffey asked himself. *'Is this man from a 1930's cop movie?'*

"Umm... yes. I have a court order for the exhumation. It's signed by a judge at the bottom if you need to verify." The man took the paper and read it. It was apparent to Brad this man had no idea what he was looking at. He looked up to Brad and nodded his head, "I'm Jimmy." Jimmy extended his hand to shake. Brad reluctantly obliged and shook. As Brad pulled his hand away, he briefly contemplated how long he should boil his hand later for proper sterilization.

"Grave's this way, we can walk on back. I got the backhoe next to the site." Jimmy motioned his head for Brad to follow, and he did. Jimmy didn't seem to care too much about walking on the graves they passed. Although Agent Duffey wasn't particularly superstitious, he had a certain respect against trampling across the dead. He minded his feet carefully as they navigated their way to the back.

"Don' get many of these diggin' orders here. This have to do with that serial killer the news keeps yabbin' about on TV?"

"Yes, well…" Brad continued to navigate the small spaces between the graves, "I can't really delve into that too much. It's still an ongoing investigation, but yes, it is in relation to that." Jimmy held up a hand, "Don't worry, I understan'… top secret." Agent Duffey shot his eyes up from the ground to Jimmy's back as he kept walking. *Top secret? It's a fucking murder investigation, not an alien abduction.'* Agent Duffey wondered if Jimmy thought the "X-Files" were a news segment.

"Here it is; I can start right away." Brad took a minute to ponder on just how the hell Jimmy got the backhoe back here before it hit him. *'Ah, of course. The bastard just drove right over the graves.'* "Yeah, that would be great. I got a van that will be here in just a few minutes to load the coffin into and take to Richmond."

"No prob 'em." Jimmy got up onto the backhoe and turned the key. It had quite a rusty start-up, but it got going in no time. Agent Duffey backed up a bit to give him the space he needed to work. Soon, Jimmy swung the arm around and began digging into the dirt that still hadn't seemed to recover from when it had been placed here upon the initial burial. Jimmy may have been an odd man, but he moved quickly and accurately with the backhoe. Agent Duffey was relieved he would be done here shortly.

Chapter 20

At approximately the same time Agent Duffey was acquainted with Jimmy from Summerset Memorial Park, Glenda Jones was strolling into work. Glenda had been a dispatcher for Emerald County Communications Center for eighteen years. Although there was a hefty list of duties and responsibilities that came along with her title, handling emergency and non-emergency calls from Emerald Residents and dispatching calls on police and fire-EMS terminals seemed to grasp most of her duty day. Glenda got into the job at the young age of nineteen. Unsure of what her future held and feeling that college life wasn't for her, Glenda didn't know where to take her life from there. Before the age of online job postings, Glenda saw a job post ad in "The Emerald Issues" for Communications Officer. Glenda figured this would be a decent job to hold her over until she could find herself and pursue her life. However, a job only meant to hold her over quickly became a career. Glenda instantly fell in love with the job and felt like it was her calling. Glenda blinked, and almost twenty years later, she was still doing the job she loved.

As Glenda entered the office, the three day-shifters were having a laugh and greeted her upon her arrival.

Although Glenda's shift didn't start until three, she chose to pick up a few hours of overtime and take over the call-taking terminal, or "the phones," as they referred to it. The current dispatcher on that terminal was taking off early for a doctor's appointment.

Glenda followed her usual routine of grabbing a soda from the vending machine in the breakroom, using the ladies' room, and then taking over. As the outgoing dispatcher unplugged her headset from the call system, Glenda plugged hers in and oriented herself, ensuring everything was ready.

Glenda's first call was relatively mundane. A local resident claimed that their mailbox was clipped by a passing car and wished an officer would respond to take a report so they could file a claim with their insurance company. Glenda entered the call into the system and submitted it to be transferred to the police terminal just a dozen feet away from hers. The dispatcher working at that terminal would summon an officer to respond. Just a moment later, the phone began to ring again, the call coming through on the 911 line.

"Emerald communications; Jones. What's the address of your emergency?"

"OH MY GOD, SHE'S DEAD! SHE'S FUCKING DEAD!" The voice of a young woman, screaming belligerently into the phone. It was pretty arduous, almost unintelligible, but Glenda still made out what she said. Glenda's heart rate began to increase slightly, but she had the experience to stay calm under these circumstances. "Ma'am, everything's going to be okay; I need you to stay calm and tell me where you're at."

"SHE'S DEAD! SOMEONE KILLED HER!"

"Ma'am, I need an address."

"THREE-FIFTY-FOUR HAMILTON, APARTMENT THREE B! PLEASE HURRY, THERE'S BLOOD EVERYWHERE! SOMEBODY KILLED HER!"

"Ma'am, the police are on the way, okay? I need you to stay calm. Are you safe? Is there someone in the house with you?"

"No..." the intensity of the voice seemed to subside. The shouting had turned into sobbing. "Okay, what is your name, ma'am?"

"Crystal... Johnson."

"Okay, Crystal, I'm staying on the line with you, but the police are on their way. The phone number on my screen is eight zero four, five five five, two six one eight. Is that the number you're calling from?"

"Yes, that's my cell." Glenda typed expeditiously, adding notes to the call as she gathered the information, which she would then relay to the officers enroute.

"Okay, Crystal, are you safe? Are you still in the home?"

"No, I'm outside on the sidewalk."

"Okay, Is there someone dangerous in the home right now? Did someone break in while you were there?" Crystal continued sobbing on the phone. "No, I came to babysit for someone... I walked in; there was blood everywhere. I found her in the bathtub. She was murdered. As soon as I saw her, I ran out and downstairs. I don't think anyone was still in there."

"Okay, Crystal, make sure you stay out at a safe distance. I will stay on the line until an officer arrives. One should be there in just a minute. If you see anyone else leave, let me know immediately so I can also let the officers know."

"Thank you." Crystal continued to sob, "Please hurry! She has a child; I don't know where he is."

Glenda continued to add the notes that Crystal relayed to her to the call in the system. It was only another minute that Glenda could hear the sirens from the first police unit arriving on scene coming through Crystal's phone.

"Crystal, I hear a siren. Do you see the officer arriving on scene?"

"Yes, I see him. He's pulling up now." Glenda could sense a touch of relief in her voice. "Okay, Crystal, since police are on the scene, I'm going to terminate the call. Please listen to the officer and take whatever direction he gives you. Good luck, darling."

"Thank you," Crystal responded with such a mixture of grief and gratitude that Glenda could only imagine what she had witnessed. Glenda disconnected the call.

Chapter 21

It was almost one in the afternoon. Detectives Bradley and Lugo arrived on location together at the apartment. They received the call shortly after the first patrol officers arrived on the scene and discovered Victoria and her son inside. Although not confirmed by anyone on scene before the detectives' arrival, it was apparent that this was another killing by the man they had been hunting.

Both detectives exited the vehicle and approached the area taped off and guarded by a few road patrols. They walked through the barrier and inside the building. As they entered, one of the few forensic investigators staffed for the Emerald Police Department was passing them on the stairs; Her face was pale with shock. Forensics always sees the worst of the worst, but nothing can prepare someone for an incident like this.

Michael was first through the door. Upon entry, a horrid scene was already in view. The living room and kitchen appeared to be in order. The nightmare began just past the hallway entry leading to the apartment's rear. The white walls and carpet were painted with blood; the carpet was matted with coagulated blood. He could see the smears on the carpet leading down the hallway; it was apparent someone had been dragged away.

Two patrol officers were in the room, silent and dismayed; they had seen horror down the hall. They both looked up at Michael and Daniel as they entered. Greetings were conducted by head nods. This was not the mood for grand welcomes.

Detective Lugo spoke first, "Has everything been photographed already?"
"Yessir," One of the patrolmen stated. Daniel nodded in acknowledgment, "Was anything touched?" The other one spoke up. "I only touched her neck for a pulse, you know? I had a glove on. The other... I already knew." Michael looked over to Daniel, "Two victims; that's new... unexpected guest?"

"Thanks, gentleman," Michael stated to the officers in the room. "If you don't mind waiting outside, make sure no one else finds their way in here unless they have a business doing so." Both patrolmen looked at each other with discontent. They knew that was code for not being wanted around. They nodded at the detectives and stepped outside.

Both detectives proceeded to the entrance of the hallway and looked down towards the end. There were three doors, two on the left and one on the right. The blood trails led to the first door on the left. They sauntered down the hallway to the entrance of the door. Detective Bradley looked inside first, revealing Victoria in the bathtub. They stepped inside, carefully avoiding the blood on the vinyl floor. Victoria was still half floating in red, murky water. The blood seemed to be mostly settling to the bottom of the tub; it was clear she had been dead for a few days. A decent amount of bloat left her buoyant in the water.

Daniel's attention was grabbed by a small piece of paper on the back of the toilet just next to the tub. "Here," He pointed to it, "his note." Michael snapped his head over to it, a small handwritten note. Michael slipped a pair of latex gloves on his hands and picked it up. He read it out loud to Daniel, "No. 7 played nicely for five, six, and seven."

"What the hell does that mean?" Daniel asked. "They said there were two victims, that would make five and six... you think there is a third one here?"

"I don't know," Michael answered in a tone of questioning options, "Let's go check the back."

They both exited the bathroom and went across the hall. The stomachs of both detectives sunk as they walked into the room. The crib answered the question of who the victim could be. With a blanket hanging over the railing, their view was mostly obscured. However, the unmistakable end of a knife handle was sticking up. Michael looked over first and immediately raised his hand up to Daniel behind him, signaling him to stop. It only took one of them to see, and Michael didn't want Daniel to see if he didn't have to.

Michael suddenly felt nauseous. He could feel his lunch beginning to regurgitate, rising inside of him at an alarming rate, and knew that he had passed the point of no return. *'Evel Knievel was at the bottom of the ramp,'* his father would always say; there was no stopping it from coming. Daniel could hear him trying to choke it back and panicked, "Not in here! You'll contaminate it!" Michael ran out, almost turning into the bathroom, then remembered the unfortunate circumstances he had been left in. He managed to hold it in until he made it to the kitchen. Just as Michael hit the sink, he let it loose. It all came out in one fell swoop. Michael ran the water and put his mouth under the faucet. He swished and spat several times, trying to rid his mouth of the foul taste.

While Michael had hurled his guts in one motion in the kitchen, Detective Lugo had foregone his warning and looked inside the crib. He had to know; he had to see. He regretted it immediately. He took a step back and closed his eyes. Letting a deep sigh out of his nose, trying to process what a sick fuck it took to do something like this. He opened his eyes and stepped back up to the crib once more to look down at the life gone too soon. He gently whispered, "Sorry."

Michael got in one last swish and pulled a paper towel from the spindle next to him on the counter. He began to wipe the water that was running down his chin and probably some loose vomit as well. He turned around and leaned on the counter to gather himself as he continued to wipe his face. Michael looked around the kitchen, which seemed clean compared to the rest; no apparent violence had occurred here. As his eyes continued to float around the room, something on the fridge caught his eye. It was immediately recognized as a string of sonogram pictures stuck to the refrigerator with a magnet, presumably, of the child in the back. Michael looked over them, picturing the journey of the boy from these pictures to where he lay in the back, but Michael quickly noticed something else. The date listed on the photo was from just a week prior. This wasn't the same child at all. The woman was pregnant. *'Five, six, and seven,"* he said to himself in his head. It finally made sense. The bastard killed a pregnant woman and a child, slaughtered like pigs.

"Lugo!" he shouted to the back. Detective Lugo came out in a hurry. "What is it? Did you find something?" "Yeah." That's all Detective Bradley could muster as he handed him the photos. Look at the date." "Jesus fuck, she was pregnant?"

"Looks like we found our seventh." Michael went over to the kitchen table and took a seat. He placed his face in his hands and rubbed his eyes vigorously. Detective Lugo walked over and said, "Let's finish this up, man. Let's do what we need here and talk to the babysitter. When the sergeant called, he said that's who found her." Michael nodded his head.

Chapter 22

Detectives Michael Bradley and Daniel Lugo exited the building back to the chaos in the street out front. Although the real horror was upstairs, it was painted in an eerie quietness. A peaceful calm seemed too inappropriate of a description for the bodies that lie above them. The true disarray was out here. Street cops running around busy with tasks from the high brass on scene, others attempting to look busy. Poor execution at that was better than no execution, Bradley assumed.

"I guess that's her," Detective Lugo nodded in Crystal Johnson's direction. Detective Bradley looked over and saw a young black female wrapped in a blanket sitting on the trunk of a patrol vehicle. His immediate thought was how beautiful of a young woman she was, but now was no time for such a comment.

"I would assume so," Bradley replied. As they approached her position, they exchanged nods with the patrol officer keeping her company. He didn't need as much hint as the others upstairs that his presence wasn't needed or wanted. He walked away swiftly without closing out whatever conversation he was having with Crystal.

"Miss Johnson?" Detective Lugo asked, "Would it be too much to ask a few more questions?"
"No, that'd be fine. Crystal is fine, as well." Crystal's eyes looked in their direction, not quite at them, but more through them.

"Daniel, please. And this is Detective Bradley, but you can call him Michael." Crystal looked up to see Michael giving an awkward smile. His way of affirming Daniel's comment. Daniel kicked off the questions. "Can you tell us what all transpired here today? From the beginning?"

"Sure," Crystal said, almost with a hint of elation. "I babysit for Victoria a few times a week. Mondays, Wednesdays, and Fridays around noon or one in the afternoon for about two hours or so. She goes to the gym before work. She works evenings, but the evening care place she takes Silas to only watches him for so many hours a day, or they charge her an astronomical amount. I take college classes in the evenings, so I watch him a few times a week during the day so she can go to the gym or the store and such for a few extra bucks. It's hard to carry a regular job, take care of my dad, and float three classes a week, so helping Victoria has also helped me." Daniel nodded and gave a "Mmhmm" to get her to continue.

"Well, today, I came upstairs like usual, but she didn't come to the door when I knocked. I called her cell, but it went straight to voicemail like it was off or dead, not typical of Victoria 'cause she stays on that phone." Crystal let out a chuckle as the tears started to flow again. "Victoria gave me a key awhile back, you know, in case I had to leave for some reason with Silas, I could lock up. Never really had to use it much. I put the key in and..." Crystal stopped for a minute and took a few long and deep breaths as if she was mentally preparing to relive the moment as she told it. "I put the key in and went inside. I got halfway through the living room before I saw the blood. It stopped me in my tracks... there was so much of it. It was everywhere. I knew I had to get out of there, but I had to find her. What if she had been in trouble or was still alive? I couldn't just leave her in there." Crystal took a few more breaths to calm herself. The tears were still running down her soft cheeks. "I crept towards the back, where the blood led to. I could see the smears leading into the bathroom. I could feel my feet getting heavier as I approached. Something inside me knew she was already dead. I had to see it, though, to believe it, to make sure she wasn't hurt and needed help. I wanted to call her name out, but I couldn't speak. I got to the bathroom door and looked in. I collapsed in the hallway, clinging to the door frame. I could see she had already gone. I knew she was past saving."

"What about the boy?" Michael interjected. "Did you discover him as well?" Crystal began to sob uncontrollably for a few seconds and then toned it back down. She snorted a glob of snot running down her lip and continued. "I had to know he was safe. I went to his room and..." the sobbing episode ended its interlude. It came back in full force. Michael looked over at Daniel, who was writing this down. Not that the discovery was particularly important, but Daniel was a fan of the details and having answers for everything.

"I saw him," Crystal said firmly as she clenched the tears. Daniel's writing led straight into the pen, dragging off the paper as he raised his head. "What?" he asked, perplexed. "There's no way he was still in there... Crystal... she's been dead a few..."

"Not today," She interrupted. "Wednesday. It was *him.*"

"Are you certain?" Michael asked. "What did you see?"

"When she came home from the gym, we exchanged our usual farewells and agreed upon the next time, for today that was. As I was leaving... he was coming upstairs."

Michael interrupted again. How do you know it was him?"

"It had to be... I ain't ever seen him before. There are only six apartments on that stairway. I've seen all of them and the usual guests from time to time. I've never seen him."

"Did he say anything to you?" Michael asked anxiously as Daniel continued his notes.

"I don't remember, honestly. Maybe hello, maybe nothing. He smiled at me, though. He had a nice smile. I thought he was handsome, but now..." She trailed off and shook her head back and forth slightly as if she were fighting off words.

"Now what?" Michael asked.

"Now, the thought of his face disgusts me." This time, Daniel piped up. What can you tell us about him? Anything and everything that comes to mind will help us get him. The smallest detail could be the most important."

"He was white, not very tall. Maybe five-nine, give or take. He had brown hair, about your length." She nodded towards Michael and then continued. "He had a beard, but it was kept nice. The mustache part was longer than the rest of the beard; it was trimmed down less than a half inch or so. His eyes were green, but... they almost seemed to glow. I thought he was handsome. That was the face of evil."

Crystal almost seemed disgusted with herself for thinking he was attractive. Daniel wrote down every word she said, even "Face of evil." Daniel liked to document everything. "Ma'am, do you think you'd be able to work with a sketch artist? It could really help us out. Get it right out to the public and on the news." Crystal nodded her head, "Yeah, I want to nail that fucker." Daniel and Michael looked at each other with the 'you good?' look. Their way of asking if they needed anything else before moving on. They then cut Crystal loose and told her to get some rest and that they would call her soon to schedule the sketch.

"Let's get back upstairs and get the real work done with forensics," Daniel stated. "Gonna need a scene sketch, measurements, check every surface for prints." Both detectives re-entered the apartment. The eerie quietness was still rampant among them. They were only there for a few minutes before they heard quick footsteps running up the stairs. Agent Duffey busted through the door before they could stop what they were doing. Out of breath, he looked around in dismay. "I came as soon as I heard. I had to wait for them to finish the exhumation..."

"It's okay," Michael said, for once looking almost glad to see Agent Duffey, "We need a favor."

"Sure, anything." Brad said, overwilling.

"You guys got a sketch artist?"

Chapter 23

Edward awoke in his room to soft music. His eyes stared at the almost pitch-black ceiling as his eyes struggled to adjust. The sound of quick half notes overlaid by a smooth saxophone aired in the room. As the tempo accelerated, it morphed into a carnival-style piece. *'Fuck, am I dreaming again?'* It seemed Edward was becoming more aware of his nightmares being just that. Edward looked around as the music continued to play. There, at the foot of his bed, he could see it; a dark figure with a pale face. It lurked behind his footboard. Edward could only see him from the nose up. His eyes seemed to be black holes that absorbed the light around them. *'Ah, is this an old friend from another dream or a new one?'*

Edward sat up hastily and scurried his back against the headboard with a blanket shield in place of his body, much like a child hiding from the infamous boogieman. The figure's face was now revealed from this angle. *'A new friend indeed.'* A grim smile that allowed a flash of teeth to show through cut through him. Edward felt as if he was in an unwinnable staring contest. He knew that thing wouldn't blink; maybe it didn't have the ability to.

Without a word, the figure turned its head to its left, Edward's right, to the corner by the door. There was another figure, just the same. Standing in the corner with its head cocked slightly to the side like a dog after calling its name. The room began to lighten. A low hue of light appeared out of nowhere, almost as if a slow-turning disco ball with colored light was above the room, but none was present.

The figure in the corner seemed to have dark orange hair and a polka-dot suit. Its body seemed to advance towards Edward but without its movement being detected. It suddenly appeared closer over and over, as if floating or teleporting a few inches at a time. The first figure behind the footboard stood, revealing a black and white striped suit. The low light exposed this one, which also had dark orange hair.

The figures began to move in unison around the room to the music louder and louder until it was unbearable. The light grew brighter to an almost blinding level. The figures were virtually dancing, like some sort of choreographed circus show. The dance seemed to be graceful and violent at the same time as they advanced towards him. Their moves were sudden jerks of the limbs. It made them appear as if a puppeteer controlled from above. Edward had no interest in meeting a puppet master that would have created these.

The room began to twist around him, spiraling into obscurity. The figure scurried too fast for Edward's eyes to track both simultaneously. The room spinning, spinning, spinning, the music blaring at a deafening level. The figures stopped in the center of the room at his footboard. They both possessed the same sinister grin as the room continued to twist around them. Their mouths began to gape wide open and let out a grating, raucous scream and lurched at him as the first figure's mouth continued to widen as if it were the whale that ate Jonah until all Edward could see was inside the abyss of it...

Edward woke up again; this time, it was real. The sun was coming in through the shades of his room. He quickly remembered the figures from before and did a security check of his surroundings. Nothing was there. Edward could feel the immense amount of sweat between his back and the bed sheets. Edward looked at the clock, ten in the morning. Edward had his counseling session later that afternoon, but no rush for that now. He turned his face back into the pillow and drifted back to sleep.

Chapter 24

It was late morning on Monday following the discovery of Victoria. Detectives had worked late into Friday night documenting everything they could and released a suspect description to the media, the first real one they've had. Detectives Bradley and Lugo came into the bullpen that morning to a long list of tips, most of which were undoubtedly false, from hopefully helpful residents doing their best to do their part.

Detective Bradley had spent most of that morning with Crystal Johnson downstairs, working up a composite of their killer. A sketch artist, courtesy of Agent Duffey, had come down from the FBI Richmond field office. Although Agent Duffey was present for the sketch drawing, he mostly lingered in the background. Not out of apathy, but a favor to let everyone know Emerald police were still in charge of the investigation. The detectives had debated at great length whether to work with Crystal right away or to give her the weekend to grieve and process some of the trauma. They decided that attempting to extract an accurate portrait of the killer may have been cumbersome right away.

Detective Bradley felt they had a sufficient sketch and sent Crystal home and told her they'd be in touch soon. He walked back up to the office cubbies and desks, where he found Detective Lugo deep into his computer screen. He trotted over and flopped the sketch on his desk. Daniel looked down, absorbed it with his eyes, and then glanced up at Michael. "That's him?"

"I guess so," Michael replied as he shrugged. "Doesn't look much like a killer to me." Daniel shrugged an eyebrow back. "Hey, they aren't all Dahmer and Bundy. I guess we should get Sergeant to approve it going out to the media."

"Yeah," Michael agreed, "and further perpetuate the cycle of bullshit tips we will receive before getting any real ones. So, what are you so engrossed with on your computer? You can't defeat the porn site blocker, trust me, I've tried." Daniel chuckled and reached over and grabbed a scanned copy of the killer's most recent note.

"The note from the apartment. It's been bothering me. I've been trying to figure out what it means." Michael picked it up and read it out loud. "No. 7 played nicely for five, six and seven. It doesn't make sense to me either, but none of them do. It's all gibberish or a game, perhaps. Might not mean anything at all." Daniel pulled the note from his hand and looked at it. "No, this one is different. The sevens... they're different."

"What do you mean?" Michael asked, confused. Daniel turned it around and pointed to it as he talked. "The first seven, as in No. 7... he used a numerical denotation for it, but the second is spelled out along with five and six. That's gotta be a hint to something."

"So, what have you found out?" Michael asked as he looked at Daniel's computer screen. "Well, not much. I've been searching 'No. 7' specifically, but a bunch of things have come up. Whiskey, skin care, Beethoven... not sure if it will get me anywhere."

"Well," Michael said tiredly, "you keep at it. I'm going to grab an early lunch; do you want me to grab you anything?"

"You going to Emerald's shittiest chicken joint again?"

"As always!" Michael proclaimed. "Then something spicy... as always," Daniel replied.

Michael gathered his things and headed out of the office. Detective Lugo stayed deep in the web searches, trying to look for anything new or something he missed in the other links. He kept repeating the note in his head. *'No. 7 played nicely for five, six, and seven. No. 7 played nicely for five, six, and seven. Played nicely... played... nicely.'*

The hair on the back of Daniel's neck began to stick up. He scrambled back to the Beethoven link and clicked it.

Multiple further links for musical tracks of Beethoven's 7th Symphony. His eyes shot up to the whiteboard across the walkway, to the green dry-erase marker that had been up there for weeks. Where he and Detective Bradley had written out every single note from the killer and analyzed it over and over. *'No. 7 played nicely for five, six, and seven.'* Daniel couldn't believe it. He looked back and forth between the notes on the board and his computer screen. It finally began to make sense to him. He pushed himself away from the computer, almost in disbelief. "Holy shit."

Chapter 25

While Detective Bradley was in line ordering a batch of some of the worst fried chicken around from a small counter in a shady gas station, Crystal Johnson was just arriving home from the Emerald Police Department. Crystal had struggled dramatically over the weekend with the trauma that she discovered. She didn't know how someone could cope, ever moving forward with an ordinary sense of life. She pondered these feelings at great length, which only led to guilt that she was even allowed to have these emotions. A young woman, a child, and an unborn were lost. There were so many events in life they would never experience. How could she feel sadness about what she had gone through?

Crystal entered her apartment and threw her keys and purse into the bowl inside the door. She walked across the room and collapsed onto the couch. She had cried so much the last few days that she didn't know if she had any tears left in her body. She lay there still on the couch. Her head turned towards the television stand. On it was a picture of Victoria holding Silas just after his birth. Another photo below was herself holding him. Crystal had felt a part of his life, watching him grow.

Crystal began to think of the things she would never experience again. The sound of Victoria's laughter, the smell of Silas' hair, the sound of cartoons during her babysitting times. All this joy and happiness was taken away by an animal. An evil being that dared to flash a smile at her.

Crystal repeatedly replayed the moment they shared in the stairwell in her mind like a movie. The video file in her brain stuck in a loop. She passes him in the stairwell, they smile, they move on, she passes him in the stairwell, they smile, they move on. She couldn't get the footage out of her head. His smile imprinted on her brain forever. *'I can't believe I thought he was handsome.'*

<u>Chapter 26</u>

It was just turning Detective Bradley's lunchtime as he strolled back into the department Headquarters. He juggled his keys and cell phone with the two large fountain drinks and a brown paper bag holding his holy grail of meals, fried chicken. The grease was soaking heavily through the bag. There was an impending sense of doom that the bottom would give way at any moment. Michael knew he needed to cut back on eating this garbage. He wasn't exactly out of shape, but he never let a carb get away either. He often told himself he would take charge of his health soon, but when deciding when to start, his mind always said, *'There's no day like tomorrow!'*

Michael had just walked inside and up the stairwell to the investigation office floor. He pushed the door open with his foot, echoing throughout the floor. Once the echo stopped, it was met by a frantic Detective Lugo.

"I'VE GOT IT! I'VE GOT IT!" He shouted across the room. Detective Bradley could see him barreling towards him with a piece of paper in his hand. In a confused state, Michael asked, "You've got what?"

"The notes!"

"What notes?" Michael asked, still juggling the items in his hands. He quickly walked over to his desk and set them all down. "The killer's notes. I've figured it out, Michael! All of them!"

"Huh? What do you mean you've figured them all out?" Michael asked, still with a puzzled look on his face.

"The notes... listen. I figured out Victoria's note right after you left, or at least I think I did. Whatever... anyway, it made sense to me finally, so I looked at the other notes, and it made me do some more digging..." Daniel paused, and

Michael wasn't sure if it was to catch his breath, which he was clearly out of for some reason, or to build dramatic suspense in effect. "IT'S ALL MUSIC!"

"What do you mean it's music?" Michael was intrigued, and Daniel had almost all his attention. However, there was still concern about the chicken going cold on the desk. "No. 7 played nicely for five, six and seven! It's Beethoven!" Michael, with a dumb look of ignorance exuding from his face, questioned, "Like the dog?" Daniel's face changed for a fraction of a second to process the stupidity, and then he corrected him, "No man, the composer. Like Beethoven? Classical music?"

"Oh right," Michael played it off like he knew the whole time. "Wait, how did you figure this out? And all the others?" Daniel grabbed the piece of paper back off his desk. "Look, he said, 'No. 7 played nicely for five, six, and seven. He said, *played nicely,*' and since he used a numerical denotation, I was fixated on figuring it out. Well... Beethoven's Seventh Symphony kept popping up in my search results. Since he said, *'played nicely,'* I started to think music, right?" He continued without giving Michael a chance to interject. "So, I looked closely at the other notes, and I could link it all to classical music pieces."

Daniel pulled another sheet of paper from his desk with a long list of scribbling on it. Debbie Robinson, 'She was most beautiful in the moonlight.' That's the Moonlight Sonata, again, a Beethoven piece. Hannah Vermond, 'Just in time for coffee.' It's a piece called "Coffee" from The Nutcracker by Tchaikovsky. Then Jessica Shire, 'If a swan must fly, she must first spread her wings.' That's from Swan Lake, another Tchaikovsky piece; you know, the ballet, right? The girl dies at the end?"

Michael didn't know what to think or say, but he could tell Daniel wasn't done. He fumbled the paper over to the back. "Shannon Reed, 'She danced the dance of death.' That's Danse Macabre by Camille Saint-Saëns. Doesn't it all make sense now?"

At this point, Detective Bradley could not abort his confusion. "I'm confused. I was gone like forty fucking minutes. How the hell did you figure all this out?" he asked, even though Daniel had just explained it. "Don't you see?"

Daniel explained, "He loves classical music. I think he's listening to it while he kills them, or at least he's dedicating the killings to these pieces, or maybe he's just using the phrases in the notes for some other reason, but this is it, dude. This is it."

"So, why classical music?" Michael asked, hoping Daniel also had an explanation for that. "Shit, I don't know man. Maybe his band teacher used to touch him or some shit and made him play this music on the trumpet or clarinet, and now he's getting revenge. Or maybe I just made that up as I answered... but regardless, this is it."

Michael had to take a seat to contemplate all of this. He looked up at the board to the green dry-erase marker and read the notes himself. It seemed so simple that he couldn't believe it, but at this point, it was more than they had in a while. He looked at Daniel, "Bro, I think we're gonna get him now. Let's tell our fed friend and see what he thinks."

Agent Duffey had disappeared after the sketch meeting with Crystal Johnson but was quickly reached by phone. The discernible sound of chewing on the phone let Detective Lugo know he had also taken an early lunch. Detective Lugo was too amped up over the discovery, and an annoyed Detective Bradley had taken the phone and given him the rundown of what had come to light. Agent Duffey seemed decently intrigued and gave a "Be right there" response to Michael through the food barrier in his mouth.

Chapter 27

"Holy fuck!" Brad Duffey stood in the bullpen of the detectives' floor, staring at the board. In just the forty-five minutes since Detective Lugo's discovery, he and Detective Bradley had written the musical pieces and their notes on the board next to the victims. Agent Duffey had been a bit skeptical on his way over that the notes had finally been solved. *'Have they really been solved, though?'* He kept asking himself.

But nonetheless, he was here in awe of what he was shown. Agent Duffey wanted to believe what the detectives were telling him. After all, it made sense and seemed to fit. It just seemed too good to be true. Just because they all deserved such a break in the case after this long doesn't mean God would give them one.

"Unbelievable. How did you come up with all of this?"

"Well," Daniel said in an almost cocky voice, "It was really just some research, some ingenuity, and a little bit of luck." The tone was full cocky now. "So what?" Brad asked, "You really think this guy likes classical music enough to kill women to it?"

"Well, we don't know if he's actually listening to it while committing the murders," Daniel answered, "but he's at least doing it in tribute or theme of the pieces. But think about it...wouldn't it make sense that he played the music during? Beautiful women, beautiful music coming together. It really elevates the pieces to him, I think."

Brad started thinking that Detective Lugo should do some moonlighting as a profiler for the Bureau. "So, where do we go from here?" he asked the Detectives. This left them staring at each other. It was apparent they hadn't gotten that far yet. Agent Duffey continued, "Alright, we'll get to that. In the meantime, Shannon Reed's funeral is this Wednesday. I think we should be there."

"You think he'll show?" Daniel asked, genuinely interested in Agent Duffey's input. "He might, a lot of these guys do. They have a habit of returning to the crime scene or funerals. It feeds them. Some seem to get off on it, the grief and destruction they've created for everyone around them."

"It's a shot worth taking," Michael interjected, "I mean, it wouldn't do us any harm anyhow. If he shows, great; if not, then we were there showing support., at least. Win-win if you ask me." Daniel stepped back into the conversation. "Yeah, but we don't even know who we are looking for. He could be a ghost, for fuck's sake. We *think* he's a white male who drives a black or red truck.

That's going to be half the congregation that shows. How will we know when we see him?"

"We'll know." Agent Duffey said with astute confidence. His eyes remained locked on a bare spot on the cheap carpeted floor. The detectives paused to see if he had anything to add to support his hypothesis, but nothing came up. "Okay then," Detective Bradley said, shrugging his shoulders modestly, "We go. Until then, let's see what we can come up with for these notes and see if it leads to anything else."

Detectives Bradley and Lugo finished their lunch and began planning for the funeral with Agent Duffey. They agreed to have some state troopers undercover in the crowd. They planned to have every scenario covered. If he showed, they were ready to nail him.

Chapter 28

Four o'clock on the dot. Edward was sitting in the lobby of Dr. Brown's office. Usually calm and sometimes apathetic to the whole therapy theme, Edward was nervous today. He didn't really know what to expect with this hypnotherapy idea. He had planned on researching it before this visit, but other things seemed to keep coming up. His right foot seemed to tap, unintentionally, on the floor. At the same time, his thumbs twiddled away at each other from his interlocked hands. His thoughts continued to wander in his head about what was to come. Through his thoughts in the background, he heard the familiar, "I'll send him in."

"Mr. Jackson," the receptionist called from behind the desk, "Dr. Brown will see you now." Edward got up and shuffled down the hallway to the office he had entered many times prior. He entered and found Dr. Brown standing this time rather than sitting as usual in his most likely overpriced leather chair. His attention was immediately shifted to the tall, slender man of the same elderly age as Dr. Brown standing adjacent to him. "Edward," Dr. Brown called eagerly, "This is Dr. Harold Kramer, a long-time friend of mine from graduate school." Dr. Kramer extended a hand to Edward. He obliged and shook. Edward's hand was met with cold, loose skin on poorly aged bones. *'The fucking Crypt keeper.'*

"Edward," Dr. Kramer gathered his thoughts, "Dr. Brown here has filled me in on some of your history. He said it might be quite therapeutic to try a few sessions of hypnotherapy. I trust he's explained some of the misconceptions to you about the process." Dr. Kramer's eyebrows were raised slightly, waiting for a response or some sort of acknowledgment from him. Edward didn't say anything but nodded his head as his eyes veered over to Dr. Brown, who was standing casually with his hands in his pockets and a concerned smile on his face.

"Well then," Dr. Kramer extended his hand towards the leather couch, "let's get started." Edward gave another nod and strolled over to the sofa. As he crossed paths with the new doctor, he gave him a joking notice: "Okay, but I'm not going to lie down." Dr. Kramer let out a chuckle that turned into a mild cough. That's quite alright; sitting will be just fine."

Edward sat down and heard the leather stretch beneath him. Rather than picking a side of the couch as usual and taking advantage of an armrest, he chose dead center. His buttocks nestled directly at the seam where the two oversized cushions met. He began to sink partly and then settled nicely. Dr. Brown had taken his usual seat, sat back, and crossed his legs with his hands perched atop his left knee. He was genuinely taking a back seat to this session. The eagerness on his face exuded that he was just as intrigued about this as Edward was. Dr. Kramer walked over to the corner where an old CD player was placed. Edward had not seen it before, indicating Dr. Kramer had brought this himself. He opened a clear plastic CD case and put an unlabeled disc in the player. He then pressed a button and light static produced itself through the speakers. It was soft and calming. The noise created an instant peace in the room.

"Edward, this is white noise," Dr. Kramer stated as he sat down, "have you ever heard of it?"

"Yes, I believe I have; just soft static, right?"

"Well, essentially, yes." Dr. Kramer said, looking at a file in his lap. Edward recognized it being the same that Dr. Brown had been writing in for months during the appointments. "This sound, the white noise, has been proven to produce a calming effect, and I quite like it when doing this with my patients. The track on the disc will play this sound continuously for an hour, although we won't be listening to it that long." He began writing notes of his own now on the page. "You see, Edward, there are different color noises that people use; there's white, pink, brown, and such. They may all sound similar to most people, and they basically are, but at different frequencies. I like to set the mood with white noise for my patients to relax. To me, it sounds like soft rain in the distance or perhaps rain off a tin roof. Can you hear that, Edward?"

"Yes." Edward suddenly felt relaxed. After all the lack of sleep, he wondered if this was what he should have used the whole time to help.

Dr. Kramer started again, "Edward, I'm going to begin the therapy session now. For this, I'm going to start by asking questions about the night your mother was killed. Dr.

Brown has gone into detail about some of your history with me and believes that perhaps the trauma suffered that night may have led to many of your daily issues and struggles. He feels that discovering the true events of that night may be priceless information in going forward with your therapy as it may give true guidance on a treatment path. Is that okay?"

"Yes," Edward answered nervously. He didn't know why he was nervous; he barely remembered anything from that night. His mind had mostly blocked it out, and he wasn't sure if this little stunt would pull it back out from the depths of his mind.

"I'm going to keep the white noise playing while I ask some questions, okay? After a few questions, I will try my best to help you unlock that night in your mind; I believe the thoughts are still in there somewhere. I will switch the white noise to something else when I get to that part. You remember me telling you the different color noises, right? The white, pink, and brown?"

"Yes, I remember." Edward could barely focus on anything other than the soft white noise playing. It was so enchanting, almost hypnotizing... *'Oh, right.'* He realized that that was the point.

"Good. Well, when I switch the track on the CD, it will be what is often called orange-peaked noise. It will be a low rumble noise that I've used in the past. I think the change in tones and frequencies will help your mind trigger itself into changing states." Edward just nodded; he was ready to begin but terrified to discover what he couldn't remember. What if he found he could have stopped it? Would he be able to live with himself? "Edward, if you would now close your eyes while I begin the questioning." Edward didn't say anything. He closed his eyes and rested his head backward until it, too, just as his buttocks, was nestled in the crevice of the leather cushions on the back of the couch.

"Edward, I believe you and your sister were in the home that night. How old were you?"
"Fifteen."
"And your sister, Elaine, is it?"
"Yes. She was twelve."

"Good, good. You were both in your bedrooms, is that correct?"

"Yes, I had just gotten into bed… I think." Edward had always remembered it that way, but suddenly, he wasn't sure of that anymore. "And your mother," Dr. Kramer continued, "was she in her bedroom, as well?"

"Yes."

"Good. You're doing fine. Do you remember seeing the man that killed your mother that night?"

"No… I mean, I don't think so… I can't remember."

"That's okay. Now, Edward, I'm going to change the track on the disc, okay? I want you to do your best to envision yourself in the bedroom that night. I want you to really dig deep and open your mind to what happened that night. Don't let a scary image deter you from digging deeper. I'm not putting you to sleep or anything crazy like they do on television. You will be here with me the whole time. The memories are just that, okay?"

"Okay." Edward did not feel okay. He was about to relive the night he had blocked out most of his life, and he was terrified of what might be discovered. His pulse was starting to rise, and his heart began a steady thump in his chest.

"Okay, Edward. I want you there... now!" Dr. Kramer simultaneously changed the track to the orange-peaked noise. The change startled Edward. The soft static changed to a low tone, almost a rumble, creating an ominous feeling inside him.

Edward felt himself almost sucked in somewhere, never leaving his seat. The noise became deafening, although the volume did not rise. That rumble. Edward was overly aware of his breathing. His breathing seemed to be the loudest in the room, like when you have noise-canceling headphones on, and your breath echoes in your head.

Edward felt himself back in his bedroom. He wasn't in bed but standing in the middle of his room. He was looking at the old, pale green carpet on the floor. Before him was the white bedroom door. The orange rumble continued. A lurking feeling of impending evil was flowing through his veins. His anxiety was maxed at this point as the creeping fear became overwhelming. He didn't want to see his mother like that again. He heard a faint voice through the loud rumble but didn't catch what it was. It took a second attempt to realize it was Dr. Kramer.

"Edward... Edward, are you there? In your house?"

"Yes."

"What do you see?"

"I'm in my room. I see the door. My bed is behind me in the corner of the room."

"Uh-huh, do you hear anything? Do you hear your mother screaming for help?"

"No. It's quiet. I don't hear anything." Edward's eyes were still closed, but he could hear the discernable sound of Dr. Kramer's pen on the pad writing.

"Okay, Edward. Do you remember going through the door? Can you see yourself going through it?"

"I don't wanna go through the door." Edward was beyond terrified now. He couldn't deal with the stress of this, reliving the trauma. Tears had begun to flow down his cheeks. He was confident Dr. Kramer could see them. Still, his willingness to continue the session made Edward question if he was more in this for himself than finding the truth to deal with the past.

"Edward, go through the door. You went through it at fifteen, so you can do it now. It's just a memory." The tears were pouring harder now. "I'm scared."

"Go. Through. The door." Edward could feel himself moving towards the door now. He reached it and turned the knob. The door opened to the dark landing between his room and his mother's.

"Okay... I went through it."

"What do you see now, Edward?"

"My mother's door."

"Have you heard anything yet, Edward? Can you hear her screaming? Someone in the house? Your sister?"

"No, it's quiet. I can feel something in my right hand."

"What is it, Edward? What's in your hand?" Dr. Kramer seemed anxious himself. Almost giddy about what was happening and discovering the past. "I don't know what's in my hand, Doctor. I can't look down. Why can't I look down?" Edward asked in a panicked voice.

"Remember, Edward, you aren't there now; it's just a memory. If you can't look down at your hand in your memory, it's because you didn't look down at it that night.

The faucets of Edward's eyes were on full blast right now. He didn't want to continue. Dr. Brown could sense the fear in Edward's voice and became greatly concerned for his patient. He decided to interject on Edward's behalf. "Dr. Kramer, maybe we shouldn't continue. Edward perhaps needs more time; I thought he was ready..."

"-he's fine," Dr. Kramer said sternly without looking away from Edward.

"Edward, go into your mother's bedroom," Dr. Kramer said forcibly. Dr. Brown tried interjecting again. "Dr. Kramer, please, I think we..."

"Shut up. He's fine." Dr. Brown was ghastly taken aback at this. He had seen something in Dr. Kramer he had never seen before, and he was even beginning to feel uneasy.

"I don't want to be here anymore, Doctor." Edward pleaded with him. Dr. Kramer did not sympathize. "Go into her room, Edward. Tell me what you see."

"Okay," Edward said hesitantly. I'm going through the door; it's dark."

Dr. Brown gave another attempt, "Dr. Kramer, I insist we stop this."

"He's fine.," Dr. Kramer said sharply, "You wanted this."

"I wanted to..." Dr. Kramer didn't let him finish. "Edward, what do you see?"

"I see my mother," Edward said in a shaken voice. The pen continued to scribble on the pad. "Edward, is she dead? Do you see someone in the room?"

"No," Edward said, confused, "She's sleeping... wait... no... NO! STOP! STOP! STOP!"

Edward frantically shouted as Dr. Brown pleaded with Dr. Kramer, "Dr. Kramer! This is extremely unethical! What the hell are you doing?"

"Shut up, you know nothing about this!" Edward continued to shout, "STOP IT! STOP IT! STOP IT!"

"DR. KRAMER!' Dr. Brown shouted alarmingly, which was still ignored. "Edward, tell me what's happening." Dr. Kramer was at the edge of his seat awaiting an answer but was interrupted by Dr. Brown once again. "DR. KRAMER! ENOUGH!" Dr. Kramer still didn't look away from Edward and was again about to ask him about the memory when Dr. Brown let out a thunderous roar. "HARRROLD!"

This got Dr. Kramer's attention. It was inescapably clear to him that Dr. Brown had no intention of letting him continue this façade. Dr. Brown looked over to Edward, who had apparently been hoisted out of the memory state by the shout as well. "Edward, are you okay?" Dr. Brown asked, genuinely concerned about his mental state. Edward caught his breath momentarily and wiped away the tear trails left behind on his cheeks. He let out a pitiful, "I think I wanna go home now." Dr. Brown nodded and saw Edward out of the office. Once gone, he turned to Dr. Kramer, who was also standing in the room; there seemed to be a show-down tension between them.

Dr. Brown made the first move. "Give me one reason I shouldn't report you to the board for this shit. That was completely unethical. This is not like you; you don't do this shit." With a smug grin, Dr. Kramer answered, "I had to with him. I had to reveal what was there. He had to be pushed further than an average patient."

"Why is that, Harold?" He asked angrily, "What is the reason that led to this fuckery?" Dr. Kramer retracted his head backward momentarily. Almost in awe that Dr. Brown didn't see what he did. "You really have no idea, do you?"

Chapter 29

Wednesday, just after one in the afternoon, Shannon Reed's burial ceremony was getting underway. Summerset Memorial Park, one of many in Emerald, was the same resting place as Hannah Vermond. That was until they decided to dig her up. Her family had apparently skipped the traditional church service and decided to only host a small gathering and service at the burial lot.

Detective Bradley, Detective Lugo, and Special Agent Duffey were all in attendance. They spent the better part of the day prior hypothesizing how they would identify the killer and planning their actions if he showed up and was identified. Ultimately, the detectives contacted Charlene

Harris, Shannon's roommate, whom they had previously questioned. The detectives had conference-called her and worked out the plan. It was known that Charlene was undeniably the most critical person in Shannon's life. If anyone could spot an outsider at the funeral that didn't belong, it was her. Of course, they had pondered the thought of long-lost relatives appearing as they often do in these circumstances. Still, it was assumed that these guests would flock to the rest of the family, efficiently eliminating them.

The plan was simple. If Charlene got 'the feeling' about someone who shouldn't be there, she would run her left hand through her hair three times. This would be the signal for the trio to act. Several state troopers were on standby just down the street, ready at the radio's call for assistance. The three had pondered having a few of them present at the park, but they didn't want to risk being spotted. The three of them had dressed relatively casually; no badges were displayed, and their guns had been inconspicuously concealed on them. Only Detective Lugo had brought a radio that was shoved into his left front pocket. Not exactly discreet, but it was the best they could do to look like they belonged. Detective Bradley made eye contact with Charlene as she approached the site. She gave a very modest head nod and nothing more, just as rehearsed not to tip anyone off who may be watching.

"Do you think he'll show?" Agent Duffey asked from behind the two detectives. Neither one of them looked back towards him. Instead, they continuously scanned the slowly growing crowd as nonchalantly as they could. "I'm not sure," Detective Bradley answered, still not breaking eyes from the crowd. But we're ready for him if he does."

The service was beginning. The pastor walked up to the front of the crowd. He stood between them and the flower-decorated casket. Shannon's mother stood beside him with a sour look of desperation but no tears. Those had all left her body weeks ago, along with most of her emotions; nothing remained inside. Detective Bradley watched the crowd intently, shifting his eyes from person to person. Everyone seemed to belong at this time, and no one was out of place. He periodically checked Charlene to see if she was sending any signals, but there were none.

Agent Duffey's phone began to ring in his pocket. Both detectives instinctively look back at him with a *'Hey, how 'bout you silence that.'* Expression on their faces. Rule number one on any stakeout mission: Never bring unwanted attention to yourself. Agent Duffey had a 'sorry' expression on his face as he pulled it from his pocket, "Hang on, I'm gonna take this." He stepped away from the group and wandered just over the berm out of sight to not disturb the masses.

Michael looked over to Daniel briefly before reverting his eyes to the crowd. "Anyone catch your fancy yet?"

"Eh... not really, how about you?"

"Me neither. Do you think he's watching from afar?" Michael looked off and around in the distance as he said this. Daniel didn't seem to think so, however. "Nah, the troopers off-site are watching with binoculars and checking vehicles. They'd hit me on the radio if they saw anything." Michael shook his head, annoyed. "I really thought he'd show. He should be here by now."

"Well…" Daniel trailed off, "Maybe he doesn't. Who knows. This was as good as any plan to catch him. If he doesn't show, another opportunity will present itself.

Agent Duffey wandered back over to the two. They did not turn to him as he stopped just short of them. "Lab called. They're done with the autopsy, second autopsy that is, on Miss Vermond." Both detectives looked back between them over their shoulders, intrigued. "You gonna keep us in suspense, Duffey?" Michael said sarcastically. "Red fiber. Located in her hair just above the base of the skull." Agent Duffey certainly had their attention now. "They compared it to the other recovered from Miss Reed; it's a match. So now, if our guy shows up and we can identify him, I'll get a search warrant for his truck, match it to the carpet fibers, and bam! Case closed."

"If he shows." Daniel butted in, "What about paint chips? Anymore located?"

"No, sorry. But the fibers should be enough. So, what's up with our guy? No-show?" Daniel didn't take his eyes off the crowd, "No, at this point, I don't think he'll show."

Thirty minutes passed, and the sermon ended. Family and friends were walking up to the casket and exchanging condolences with Shannon's mother and Charlene. It was apparent the target was a no-show. The crowd began to dissipate to their vehicles. Charlene looked across the green to Michael with a sorrowful, helpless look. Her face was bitter. This bastard had taken a life so dear to her and didn't even give a shit enough to show.

The three gentlemen walked back towards their cars as well. Agent Duffey was half seated in his vehicle as Michael and Daniel were just opening their doors to the car they shared over. "Hey guys!" He called out to grab their attention. "I almost forgot. Might be something, might be nothing." He walked over to them and pulled out his phone to show them a clip he saw on social media. The picture showed several violinists seated in a row, mid-piece. "The Richmond Symphony is playing a concert this Friday in the city." Daniel and Michael exchanged excited looks across the top of the car. Daniel, from the other side of the car, couldn't see the flyer on Agent Duffey's phone. "What are they performing?" When Agent Duffey answered, Michael's stomach fluttered with anticipation. This was it. The bastard was going to show. Agent Duffey looked up from his phone across the car to Michael and answered. "Beethoven's 7th."

Chapter 30

Edward awoke from a shallow sleep a few hours after Shannon's funeral had ended. After the nightmare therapy session with the psychotic doctor, Edward wasn't sure if he would ever have a sound sleep again. Since that session, Dr. Brown has called and left several voicemails on his phone. He sounded deeply sorry for his friend's behavior. He even offered to report him to the medical board if Edward wished. Disregarding his thirty-year friendship with Dr. Kramer for his patient seemed awfully noble to Edward. Still, he had not returned any of the calls. Edward was genuinely shaken by what he saw in that session and what Dr. Kramer brought out. Edward spent the last forty-eight hours blocking out what he saw, telling himself it wasn't true. How could it be? How could he block something like that out all these years? Edward also spent the last thirty-six hours on the sauce as an extra helping hand. He woke up ready for another drink yet again.

Edward had not been at the funeral earlier that day. In fact, he had no idea the funeral had taken place. To him, Shannon was already a blip in his mind. She was too far back for him to still enjoy. He retained no interest in keeping up with the following events with his 'girls.' Edward had a habit of masturbating to them for about a week after each kill. After that, they grew stale in his mind.

He got out of bed and went to the bathroom to let out a well overdue piss; no caution in avoiding the rim and creating a backsplash on the floor around the toilet. Edward skipped the wash and went back and retrieved the empty rock glass from the nightstand. Noticing the empty bottle of bourbon next to it, he wrestled with his hangover and walked into the kitchen. He usually kept the liquor in the cabinet above the fridge. This proved useless. He had gone through it all. Edward knew he needed to clear his head but also a drink. He wasn't sure if he was ready for another adventure yet. He was still riding the wave of Victoria in his mind. But how could he pass it up if the right opportunity presented itself? He pondered this thought in his mind for a bit before deciding. *'Benny's it is.'*

Just forty-five minutes later, Edward pulled into the lot and shut his truck off. His boots shuffled across the dusty pavement that was in desperate need of attention. He walked through the doors and was hit with the same aromas as before, triggering delightful memories of Shannon. He looked to his right, where they had previously sat. He could picture her there, pretty and lonely, easy prey for a predator.

Edward looked around and saw only two other gentlemen in the joint. Both were seated to the bar's far left, with nappy beards and camouflaged hats. Neither spoke a word; both were fixated on the television featuring some sort of 'smoke-off' competition. Edward gathered about five seconds of the program that showed less than in-shape men throwing pork at smokers. He approached the semi-attractive girl working at the bar and ordered an old-fashioned. Edward wondered where the big, burly man was running the bar last time. He didn't pay it much attention.

Edward watched the woman make a sorry attempt at his drink. He took it, threw a few bucks in the plastic jar labeled 'tips,' and took a seat at an all too familiar table.

Slightly disappointed in the lack of a crowd, Edward sipped his drink. His true intention was to get his bourbon fix, but he found himself slightly annoyed with the absence of opportunity. He shrugged it off. There was always a chance of something turning up later.

Benny Davenport was in the back office of the bar. He had spent most of the day at his desk and computer, reviewing inventory, ordering new stock, and closing out overdue invoices. Benny proved to be quite a procrastinator with the administrative and logistical tasks of running the bar. This isn't exactly what he dreamed of almost twenty years ago when he opened it, but he learned quickly it was necessary to keep the dream alive.

Stacey Dunlop, the woman working the bar, was Benny's part-time employee. Her husband traveled out west frequently to work in the oil fields for weeks or months at a time. With no children at home, she found herself bored of home life. With the money her husband made, work was not a requirement of hers but rather something to do. She had worked for Benny the past few years during the stints when her husband was gone. Stacey had just finished fixing an old fashioned for a customer she did not recognize. She was used to the usuals every week, sometimes daily. However, it was not unusual for a new face to make an appearance here and there. Stacy went under the bar to grab a few more bottles to replace those thinning out on the shelf behind the bar. She noticed the stock down there was thin as well. She wandered to the back for assistance. Stacey was rather petite and had a bad back that stemmed from a high school cheerleading accident. Although she could still muster the strength to haul the cases of bottles from the stock room to the bar, Benny insisted she let him. Primarily out of kindness but also due to an on-the-job injury being the last thing this bar needed.

She popped her head into the office. "Hey, case of bourbon, two cases of vodka up front when you get a chance?"

"Yeah, no problem, Stace." He replied kindly but without looking away from his calculator as he typed. He finished his current invoice and pushed away from the desk. He stood and stretched his tight back by bending backward. He straightened up and pulled his shirt that had ridden over his belly back down. He wandered to the back and grabbed a case of bourbon bottles. Each case was pre-loaded with several brands of customer favorites, all bottom-shelf quality around here, nothing too fancy for the guests of Emerald.

Benny came through the swivel door from the back to the bar, and his heart stopped. *'Him! It's Him!'* The realization almost caused Benny to drop the case of bourbon. He quickly caught his grip. The abrupt struggle to hold his load caught Edward's attention. The two locked eyes for a few seconds. An awkward exchange of looks. Benny quickly gathered himself and gave him a friendly nod and a smile. Benny took long, deep breaths as he stocked the bar. He fought every urge to look over to the man. He felt a need to look and assure himself it was him, but deep down, he knew. Benny held his eyes on his work so as not to alert him. He planned on finishing his task and then sneaking back to his office to call the police. 'I've *got you now, fucker!'*

Edward had just finished taking the last swig of his drink when the big, burly bartender he remembered before busted through the door from the back. He had stumbled over his own feet but recovered quickly. Edward locked eyes with the man for a moment before continuing his work. *'Did he recognize me?' Does he remember me from before?'* Edward assured himself that wasn't the case. After all, so much time had passed. *'Shannon and I were just two random customers in the bar that night, right? He didn't pay any attention to us.'*

As the burly bartender continued his work, Edward felt his nervousness rise; something was off. The man behind the counter seemed to be sweating and breathing heavily. He was a massive man to be whopped by one box of booze. His attention to his work almost seemed forced on Edward. *'He's making a point not to look at me. I'm getting the hell out of here,'* Edward thought.

Edward stood up slowly and began to make his way to the door. He made it halfway when Benny's attention could no longer be diverted. His head snapped up from behind the bar, and the two again locked eyes. Benny stood up fully behind the counter. The two stood silently in a dual-style standoff, neither with a weapon to draw. Benny whispered, not so quietly, "You fucker."

'Aw, fuck.' That's all Edward needed to hear. The man remembered him and knew what he had done. Without another second of hesitation, Edward made his break for the door. He sprinted towards the exit, hip-checking every chair and table on the way. The pain was no burden on his stride. He had to get the hell away from here. As he was exiting, he could hear the large man tumbling over the bar, causing a few glasses to launch and shatter on the floor. Benny wasted no time running to the end of the bar to use the exit. He would not let the bastard get away.

"YOU FUCKER! YOU'RE FUCKING DEAD!" Benny rampaged his way out the front door of the bar. By this point, Edward had made it to his truck. He looked back as he opened the door and exchanged one last eye lock with the large man still barreling towards him. Edward started the truck and backed up as the man made it to the door, beating on the window and pulling at the door. *'Please hold.'* Edward prayed the old glass would not give. He threw the shifter into first and floored it out of the parking lot. The large man gave chase to the end of the lot.

"YOU FUCKER! I FUCKING GOT YOU! I'VE GOT A CAMERA NOW! YOU HEAR THAT? YOU'RE FUCKED!" Benny continued to scream at the man in the truck until it drove out of sight. He bent over with his hands on his knees to catch his breath and then walked back inside. He marched straight to his office, picked up the phone and dialed.

Chapter 31

Detective Bradley and Detective Lugo were on scene at Benny's within the hour. Benny Davenport had called 911 from the parking lot as the unidentified man, at least to them, fled the lot. Patrol officers on duty were dispatched to canvass the area but to no avail. Edward had exited the area rapidly, and with only six officers on shift at a time covering a decent-sized county, the odds were not in their favor.

The detectives strolled across the same dusty lot that Edward had just crossed an hour before. "You think he actually has something?" Daniel asked Michael in an unconvinced tone. "Sergeant Lewis said dispatch advised he had footage when they notified him this time," Michael responded as he shrugged his shoulders, assuming it was possible but also unsure himself. Daniel didn't respond. They both got up to the door and went inside. Benny was on the other side of the bar, leaning over on it. He turned his attention to the door as he heard it shift open.

"Offi... Detectives, sorry. Thank you for coming. That fucker was in here again." Daniel pulled out his pocket-sized notebook as Michael engaged in the questioning. "You're absolutely certain it was him?"
"Yes, of course!"
"Tell us what happened," Michael responded. Daniel had his pen ready at the pad. "Well, I was in the back. Stacey, the bartender, asked me to help her load some stuff up under the bar. I grabbed a box and came out. I saw him as soon as I

walked through the door and recognized him instantly. Fucker was even sitting at the same goddamn table." The pen on Daniel's pad was scribbling steadily as Benny talked. Michael continued with the questioning. "What happened next?" Benny looked over to where the incident had occurred as he spoke as if replaying it in his head to revive the memory. "Well... nothing at first. I came out, and I saw him, right? It kinda startled me at first. I wasn't expecting him, you know? Never thought he'd show his face again. Some balls on that guy, right?"

"And then?" Michael interjected to get him back on track. He looked at Daniel's pad to inquire if he was keeping up. He was. "Right," Benny said and cleared his throat. "So, I saw him, it kinda made me panic at first. I didn't really know what to do. I was just gonna play it cool, you know? Act like I didn't see him. I was gonna do my work and then sneak to the back to call."

"Dispatch told our Sergeant he fled. Did he know you called?" Michael asked. "Well..." Benny said hesitantly, "Things didn't go quite to plan."

"Mmhmm... and how did they go exactly?"

"I was bent over, putting the bottles away. I could feel him looking at me. Did you ever know when someone was looking at you? Even though you weren't looking at them. It was like that. I did everything I could to not look over, but..." Benny was speaking regretfully, hating himself for letting the stranger getaway. Daniel's pen caught up with Benny's words. He looked up from his pad, "What happened next?"

"I heard him get up and start walking towards the door. I guess he knew I was on to him about something. Once I heard him moving, I couldn't help myself anymore and looked at him."

"Did he see you looking?" Michael asked.

"Oh yeah... It looked like he was staring right at me, almost through me. He stopped dead in his tracks for a second and stood there perfectly still, like a statue. His soulless eyes looking into mine. The next thing I knew, he was running for the door. Quick fucker, of course, I'm no athlete." Benny patted his round belly as he finished his remark. Daniel raised his left eyebrow slightly as his tilted head nodded in agreement.

"Okay," Daniel said, looking over the notes he took. "After he took off, what happened? Did you get his vehicle? Plate?"

"I got you, man." Benny walked to the cash register and pulled a piece of yellow paper from the counter. It appears that Benny had his own notes. "Black truck, Ford F-150. Late eighties or early nineties. Large tires, maybe thirty-three to thirty-five inches. Stock rims. Had the locking hub style wheels." Michael and Daniel looked at each other excitedly. This was the break they had been holding out for, and now it was here. "What about his plate? Were you able to get that?"

"I got some of it, but not all, sorry. I was trying to do my best, but too much was going on to remember all of it." He held out the paper for them to read. "U, C, and Y are the first letters. I didn't get the numbers that followed." Michael could hear Daniel talking under his breath as he wrote, "Union, Charles, Yankee." Michael was getting antsy with what they were gathering.

"We were told you have a camera now, too? One that faces the seating area?"

"Sure do. I apologize; it's not the best, but the best I could afford." Benny led the detectives to the back office, where his monitor screen was for the cameras. Benny already had the footage set up for them. Benny had really learned to get his shit together from the last time they had an exchange with him.

"I have it starting from when he pulls up. The camera inside will slightly catch him pulling into the lot through the front window, but it's mostly good for when he comes in." Benny played the tape, and they all watched in silence. The video, which was not of decent quality, showed the bottom half of a box-style truck pulling into the far back row of the lot. Daniel tried squinting to see if the plate was readable. It was not. A second later, a white male in a black jacket, boots, and aviator-style sunglasses is seen shuffling across the lot. He momentarily disappears off camera and then re-appears as he arrives inside. The white male removes his sunglasses and pauses as he looks around to the mostly empty bar. The bartender, Stacey, is seen coming in and out of view on the bottom right of the screen. They all watched the rest of the story unfold just as Benny had told it. The tape finished with Benny chasing him out of the bar.

Detective Bradley and Detective Lugo looked at each other momentarily. They finally had a shot. "What do you think?" Michael asked Daniel. "I think it's the best break we've had so far. The footage is still a little grainy, though." "Yeah," Michael agreed, "If the footage was of him committing a crime, it wouldn't hold up in court for us to testify that it's surely him, whoever he is. But it's nothing we will have to testify to. I think it's fine for us to use it to identify him; maybe get his picture out there. Someone will recognize him." Michael focused his attention on Benny, "Can you print a picture from the footage? Preferably one with a good face shot in it?"

"Sure, no problem." Benny went to his desk computer to complete the task.

"So, what now?" Michael asked Daniel. He was so anxious that he wasn't sure what the next move should be. Let's get the picture back to the office, show Agent Duffey and Sergeant Lewis what we got, and we can plan from there," Michael acknowledged with a simple nod.

"Here you go." Benny handed over the printed still picture from the computer. The image was slightly more pixelated than on screen, but it would do for now. "Anything else you can think of?" Detective Lugo asked Benny. "Not right now, but I'll be sure to let you know if I think of anything." The detectives began to leave when Michael suddenly stopped and turned back to Benny again. "Wait, one more thing... you said when he fled that you watched him get into the truck, correct?"

"That's right," Benny said, unsure where the question was going. What color was the inside of his truck?" Benny didn't hesitate for a second to answer. "It was red. Bright red." Michael felt the flutters in his stomach again.

The detectives thanked Benny and shook hands. They were exceptionally pleased with his work this time. They walked back to their vehicle in the parking lot. "Well, let's head back over to the station and get to work," Michael said without acknowledging Daniel. He was already deep in thought, planning their next move. Michael started up the car and left the property.

Back inside the bar, Benny had gotten back to work. He finished stocking the bottles he had intended to stock earlier. He then pulled a semi-clean rag from a bucket of bleach water and began wiping down the bar top with it. He had a grin of satisfaction on his face. He felt like he had redeemed himself for letting Shannon down. However, the smile faded as he wiped, and the tears returned for his friend.

Chapter 32

It was getting late into the evening on Wednesday now. Detective Bradley was thinking of how he should be in his recliner with half a cold beer and half stale chips. But here he was, dealing with this shit. Although they finally got the break they had longed for, this case was starting to wear on him physically and mentally. Hell, it was killing all of them inside slowly.

Michael and Daniel came back into the office. Special Agent Duffey and Sergeant Lewis were in there, doing little of anything at their desks. Sergeant Lewis had initially intended to meet both detectives at Benny's to see what was discovered; however, he decided to forego that and wait at the office. He did not like to give his detectives the feeling that he was interfering with their cases or micromanaging them. He knew his detectives were solid and let them do their job mostly uninhibited. Sergeant Lewis was a stellar supervisor and was heavily respected by everyone in the investigation division.

Sergeant Lewis saw the detectives entering the bullpen and didn't give them much time to settle in. He was just as anxious as them for a break and to solve this thing. "What did you guys get?" Daniel opened his folder with the notepad and pulled out the printed picture. "Well, this for starters." Sergeant Lewis stared at it intensely in disbelief. He was finally seeing the ghost they had all been chasing for months. "Damn... this is really him?"

"We think so." Michael said assertively, "We got some vehicle information but not a whole plate." Agent

Duffey joined in, "What do you get on the vehicle?" Michael looked to Daniel to find the answer in his notes, even though he was sure he could recite them himself. Daniel opened his writing pad. "Black truck confirmed, not red. Square-body, Ford. Late eighties or early nineties. And get this…" Daniel gave a pause for suspense, "Red interior."

"It's really him, huh?" Sergeant Lewis asked no one in particular. His eyes were still fixated on the picture.

Agent Duffey chimed back in, "You said only a partial on the plate?"

"Yeah…" Michael answered, "And we need a full plate to run through VCIN or NCIC."

"That's okay." Agent Duffey assured him. "I've got a few other databases that we can run a partial plate through to see if there are any matches, but that's only if his vehicle has been entered for something before. If he's clean, there might be nothing."

Agent Duffey extended his hand to Sergeant Lewis, gesturing for the printed picture. Sergeant Lewis handed it over. "The picture isn't super great; it's a little grainy, but I guess it will do. I can send this to my office media contact;

she'll ensure the local networks get it out tonight on the late nighttime slots." Daniel began to ponder something in his mind but didn't speak at first.

Sergeant Lewis was not looking forward to the phones ringing off the hook the next few days for the hundreds of baseless tips coming in that would lead nowhere. "I hope one of you plans on staying by the phone in the office the next few days. We need a dedicated tip collector for when they start rolling in; the others can investigate them and filter out their validity." No one spoke up. There really wasn't a lesser of two evils between those tasks.

Daniel finally spoke up. "Wait..." Everyone looked over to him. "I think we should hold off on putting that picture out to the media." The three others in the group looked puzzled and waited for the follow-up to support his statement. Daniel walked over to the board and pulled off the sketch drawing that had been completed prior with Crystal Johnson. "We still haven't put this out yet, right?" "No," Sergeant Lewis answered, "I haven't sent it to the networks yet to put out. Honestly, now that we have the picture from Benny's, I don't think it's even super close. I'm sure the witness was dealing with lots of trauma when she helped render it."

"Exactly," Daniel said. So right now, we're the only ones who know what he looks like other than Benny. He might not even know for sure we have this picture."

"So, what's your point?" Agent Duffey asked. "Look," Daniel stood up from sitting on the desk as he spoke, "What if we post this picture to the news, and he goes into hiding? If he knows we are looking for him, he might not show his face again for some time." Sergeant Lewis shook his head. "It doesn't matter; someone will recognize him regardless. Then we will know who he is. He can't hide forever." Daniel still disagreed with the method. "But what if he bolts? What if he leaves town? The State? Shit, even the country? If he thinks the jig is up, he could disappear for good."

"So, what are you proposing?" Michael asked. Daniel could see everyone needed a good answer to go along with him. He looked over to Agent Duffey. "Brad, you showed us that ad for the concert on Friday, the one for the Beethoven rendition. You really think he might show to that?" Agent Duffey half shrugged his shoulders with his head tilted to the side. "I mean, I think it's as good a guess as ever. If they are playing the seventh symphony and you're right about those notes..."

"I am," Daniel said with sincere confidence. "Then I think he will," Brad said, also confidently. "Then I think we should keep the picture to ourselves and go to the concert venue. If he makes an appearance, we can identify him from the picture and grab him. We have enough to bring him in for questioning, and I'm confident we can get a search warrant for his truck, maybe even his house, once we identify him."

Sergeant Lewis was still not on board. "I don't know if I like that. What if we wait, and he kills again before then, and we could have stopped it? Could you live with that? I don't think I could. Not to mention, if it was discovered we had this and didn't act, our careers would be shot."

"I don't think he's going to kill again yet," Daniel said, shaking his head as he spoke. "I think he's still on a high from Victoria. I think it would be at least another week or two before he would even start looking for another victim. I don't see why he would break away from his pattern now."

"Can we even identify an actual pattern?" Michael asked. "Not exactly," Daniel replied, "But a general one he's been following. There seems to be at least a few weeks between each kill, and it's just been a week since Victoria. I think we've got time."

"I don't know." Sergeant Lewis said, still sounding unsure of everything. He looked back up to Agent Duffey. "What do you think Brad?" Agent Duffey pondered it for a few seconds before committing to an answer. "I think both sides are valid, and either choice could help or hurt us, but I trust Daniel's instincts. I really do." Detective Lugo gave him a slight nod as a thank you. Sergeant Lewis let out a big huff. "Alright, don't make me explain to my wife why I lost my pension." Daniel smiled; he got his green light. "Don't worry, you won't." Sergeant Lewis let out a slight chuckle. "I hope you're right. And you better have a solid plan, Alright?"

Chapter 33

It was a bit past 5 p.m. on Friday, and Edward was in his bedroom preparing for his evening out. He stood in front of his long bedroom mirror propped in the corner. He observed himself with great admiration; a black-on-black tuxedo, not a piece of white on him. Edward wanted to look sharp as this was a special occasion. The Richmond Symphony was performing Beethoven's 7th, one of his favorite pieces. And it was just after the occasion of Victoria. *'How fitting it seems,'* Edward thought to himself. Everything seemed perfect. One more adjustment on the tie, and it was good to go. Edward picked up his ticket and felt his stomach flutter with excitement. He gathered his things and left the house. The show started promptly at 8 p.m., and he had a bit of a drive to the city. Once in the truck, Edward felt that maybe driving in his tux jacket wasn't the best idea. *'Nobody wants a wrinkled tux.'* He walked around to the passenger side and gently laid it across the seat to not create a crease or fold. He walked back around, got in, and fired up the engine.

"What the fuck is this thing?" Detective Bradley asked Detective Lugo, holding up a strangely shaped piece of black fabric. "It's a cummerbund," Daniel replied in confusion, not understanding how Michael had never seen one before. It was clear that Daniel's answer did not halt Michael's confusion. "What the hell do I do with it?"

"It goes around your waist."

"Like a belt?" Michael was still staring at it in his hand like a dead animal. "No, it goes over your belt. Have you ever worn something nice outside of work before?"

"Like my Harley jacket?" Michael said with a shit grin on his face. Daniel rolled his eyes jokingly. "I should have made you get dressed at your house."

"Your place is much cleaner; plus, I'm out of beer." Michael joked.

Sergeant Lewis had allowed the detectives to play out their plan. They, too, were going to attend the Shockoe Theatre. On Thursday, the detectives went out and rented cheap tuxedos. They didn't fit quite right, but they would have to do. The plan was simple. They each had a copy of the picture pulled from Benny's in their pockets. They had tickets to the venue, not great ones, but they would do their best to watch the crowd to see if they could identify the ghost man. Neither of them truly needed a copy of the photo with them, as they had stared at it relentlessly for the past forty-eight hours.

"How do I look?" Michael asked hesitantly as he looked down at himself. Daniel turned and looked at him up and down. "Your cummerbund is upside down." Michael ripped it off from around his waist. "Alright, that's it. I'm not wearing it."

"Can we go now? We're gonna be late." Daniel was looking at his watch impatiently. Michael responded in a feminine voice, "Oh Hun, you always rush me." They both shared a laugh. Daniel and Michael had always been great friends, but working closely on this case for so long brought them closer together. They had started to feel like true brothers to each other.

"You heard from Brad?" Michael asked Daniel. "He and Sarge are already headed up in the van; I don't want them to catch him without us." Other than the two detectives, Sergeant Lewis and Agent Duffey were the only backup they would have. They wanted to keep this small and quiet. Too many officers, even plain clothes, can give it away. They knew the killer was clever. He could easily pick out someone in each corner of the venue looking at the guests with seemingly no interest in the show. "Alright," Michael said, "let's do it."

It was close to 7:30 p.m. as Edward was shutting off his truck. There was no direct parking at the Shockoe Theatre, so he had to pay for a spot in a public parking deck a few blocks away. The air was crisp and cool, so he did not mind the walk. His dress shoes made a distinctive *'clack'* against the sidewalk as he strolled alongside the road. Edward looked around and absorbed the sights. He was not very fond of the city; he never was. It is too crowded for comfort and constant noise. The Shockoe Bottom district in the city had seen better times. Once, a vibrant part of the city was now dark and dirty. Edward supposed the city was doing what they could to restore it. However, he hadn't been to this district in the city for some time and wouldn't be able to identify any progress if there had been. Edward was once fond of a landmark pizza joint in these parts but wasn't sure if it was still open.

Edward finally reached the Shockoe Theatre, and it was quite a sight to see, a much better venue than he had attended a few weeks prior in the city. A much better performance was in the forecast, as well. Unlike the community symphony filled with what Edward referred to as the has-beens and washouts, the Richmond Symphony was home to professional musicians. He had seen them perform before several times, and there was never a letdown.

Edward walked into the venue's front door and showed his ticket to the doorman. He thanked him for coming and told him to enjoy the show. The inside was awe-inspiring, white marbled floors with strips of red velvet carpet. The walls shared the same marble complexion with giant gaping windows outlined in thick gold trim. The chandeliers were also gold with crystal accents. Edward didn't usually care for the ostentatious adornment, but for this occasion, it seemed fitting. The vibrant luster was a nice change of scene from the dull white plaster walls and faded

wood plank floors. To Edward, those things were quite
alright for him, but so was this.

"Union, Charles, Yankee... Union, Charles, Yankee...
Union, Charles, Yankee..." Michael was whispering to himself
in the passenger seat. "Would you stop saying that? You're
not gonna see the truck." Daniel scoffed. Michael averted
his attention from his window to Daniel in the driver's seat.
"He's gotta park somewhere, right? Good chance we drive
right past it on the side of the street. Who knows, maybe he
will still be in it, and we can snag him right then and there.
Then I don't have to watch this snooze fest." Michael said
annoyingly as he tugged at his collar, which was half an inch
too small. He finally gave up and undid the top button to
allow himself to breathe. He pulled down the visor mirror
and tried to adjust his tie to hide the open collar. "There's
no parking at the venue, Michael, and spots are scarce here.

He could be anywhere in a ten-block radius. You wanna waste our time scouring all that?"

"Not particularly," Michael grunted. "Besides," Daniel said while reading his GPS, "There's only parallel parking around here anyway. Do you think he could fit that truck in one of these spots in between the compacts and electrics? He's probably in one of the parking garages around here. They hold a few thousand each, easy. Needle in a haystack."

"Would you just park already? I'm getting antsy. I can't breathe in this damn sweatsuit. You should have no problem parallel parking this heap of shit, either." Michael was already re-adjusting his tie, certain it looked despicable.

Agent Duffey and Sergeant Lewis sat in a white surveillance van across the street from the venue. With a large banner on the side that read "Allen's painting and Flooring" and dark tinted windows, the two could see out without anyone seeing inside. The van contained hidden cameras throughout the exterior that fed feed to a CCTV and two laptops inside.

Agent Duffey was currently taping a copy of the ghost man's photo next to one of the blacked-out windows. He pressed the tape firmly against the felt lining on the van wall. Sergeant Lewis was adjusting the camera angles from a laptop to catch the front of the venue where a long line of guests stood to get their tickets checked, as well as multiple angles of approach to the venue. "There. That should be good enough," he said to Agent Duffey. Brad looked away from the window to his laptop, which shared the same feed as Sergeant Lewis' and the CCTV. "Yeah, that'll do. I'll keep an eye on the line going in if you wanna keep an eye on the approach angles." Sergeant Lewis nodded in agreement. "Works for me. You think he made it inside before we got set up?" Agent Duffey looked at the long line out front. "It's possible; there's a fair amount of people inside already. It'll be one hell of a bitch trying to spot him in the flood of people leaving when it's over."

"Don't worry, if he's in there, my guys will spot him." Agent Duffey lifted a camera with a heavy zoom lens and began to scope the faces of the line individually. "I hope so." Brad then noticed the two detectives approaching and getting into the line. Michael, of course, had to look directly at the van and wink. Brad rolled his eyes. "They're here."

Edward made his way to his seat. The black metal seats were lined with soft red cushions that matched the carpet in the halls and the walkways. Although quite elegant, he thought it may soon be due for an upgrade. The seats in the venue formed a semi-circle around the stage below. Edward's seat wasn't the best, but they weren't the nosebleeds either, not too bad for a forklift driver. It wasn't too long before Edward was squished between the guests on either side of him. One was a rather portly fellow, and the other was a petite woman. Still, even on her side, he would fight for the armrest.

"Where the hell are our seats?" Michael asked, looking down at the tickets. "Just ask the usher in the aisle," Daniel said, pointing to the gentleman in the red button-down coat. The detectives approached him and showed them their tickets, and the gentleman in red showed them to their aisle. Before heading down to their seats, Michael stopped Daniel by putting his hand out to the side. "What's wrong?" Daniel asked, confused. "Just taking a look," Michael replied, looking into the gallery, "He's here. I can feel it."

"You want him to be here, so do I. Don't look too intently; you'll give us away."

"Just a gander, that's all." Michael took a few more visual passes over the crowd before walking to their seats. Daniel was now looking, too. "There must be eight hundred seats in here, and they're filling up fast. Judging by the line outside, there won't be many empty chairs either." Michael grimaced at his statement. "Who the fuck enjoys this shit?" Daniel looked at him and said sarcastically, "Wow, you're so cultured." They both shared a chuckle. Michael looked at his watch, "Only ten more minutes before the show starts. Once that happens, the lights will be dimmed, and spotting him will be even harder. We should have gotten more officers involved."

"Who? City P.D.? They don't give a shit about our problems. They can barely take care of their own. Besides, how many officers do you think they'd spare for two rural detectives who think there is a possibility a killer *might* show up?"

Michael pondered his answer for a moment. "Yeah, I guess you're right. I hope Brad and Sarge jump in if anything goes down."

Edward was sitting across the gallery from where the detectives had entered. He was casually people-watching as usual; People of all backgrounds were in attendance. Hundreds of years of history behind this music had captured the ears of all types. As Edward looked upon the crowd, his eye was caught by something. Across the gallery, almost entirely opposite him in reference to the position of the stage, two gentlemen had entered. One white and one Latino. Edward noticed the white male seemed to be peering into the crowd around him. The Latino man said something to him, and they went to their seats. Edward didn't think too much else about it. Edward looked down at his watch. The show was about to begin, and he could barely contain his excitement. The lights dimmed, and the musicians flooded from the tunnels to their chairs. The crowd started to applaud; Edward included.

Back in the van, Agent Duffey and Sergeant Lewis were meticulously scanning the guests in line. The line had thinned out significantly over the past twenty minutes, but a fair amount stood in wait. "I'm not getting anything over here. Are there any possibilities on your side?" Agent Duffey asked Sergeant Lewis, who was peering into a pair of binoculars through the windshield from behind the driver seat. "No one that's caught my eye. Think this guy is a no-show?" Agent Duffy was chewing on his bottom lip in frustration, thinking the situation was over. "I don't know, man. It's possible, but it's also possible he was already inside before we got set up." Sergeant Lewis pulled the binoculars from his face and hunched his back to stretch it, feeling instant relief. "You wanna poke our heads inside? An extra pair of eyes or two might not hurt."

"No..." Agent Duffey shook his head modestly, "I don't want too many people in there looking around. Besides, if they spot him and make a move, I want to be out here in case he bolts."

Agent Duffey felt his phone vibrate in his pocket. He dug into it with his left hand and pulled it out. The front screen showed it was a text from Michael. He unlocked his phone to read the text message. It simply read, 'Show's starting.' Agent Duffey looked back up to Sergeant Lewis, "It's starting. The waiting game continues." Brad Duffey sent a text message to Michael, 'Don't get lost in the music.' A moment later, another text message returned to his phone, 'Won't be an issue.'

The music was beginning, and Michael was agitated, to say the least. The music made his ears want to bleed. He scanned the crowd intently, taking brief breaks to look down on the musicians with disdain. At first, he was randomly scanning the faces around him, then across from him, but that proved quite cumbersome. He then switched strategies to starting at the top row of the venue across from him and attempting to move down each row individually; this proved equally challenging. Too many faces were blurring together, and the lighting was only decent near the musicians. Michael caught several faces that made him double-take before mentally crossing them off his list.

Daniel was not bothered or distracted by the music. He had tuned it out. He was focused on the crowd, as well. The venue could have been silent to him, and he would not have known the difference. He reached into his pocket and pulled out a folded-up picture of the killer. He frequently looked down at it between looking at different sections of people. He wanted the image to be as crisp in his mind as possible. Daniel knew the killer was here; his senses felt it when they entered the venue. Daniel would stay focused on the crowd the entire set if needed. If the killer was here, he was not going to get away.

Edward was so enthralled by the music he was grinning from ear to ear. He had seen many classics performed over the years, but after a rendition of just two pieces, he knew this would be one of the top performances. There was another slight pause in the music, and Edward joined in a crowd of applause as the musicians changed their sheets to the next piece. As the music picked up again, his attention broke and drifted to the crowd. Something peculiar caught his attention. The two gentlemen he had seen earlier looking into the crowd. Both the white man and Latino were peering all over the seated guests and paid virtually no attention to the crowd. Again, believing he was overthinking the situation, Edward focused back on the music. Within seconds, his attention was averted back to the strange men. *'Who are you looking at? Who are you looking for?'* Edward did his best not to pay them any mind, but he found himself shifting his eyes from the performers to them every few seconds. The more he saw them looking around, the more nervous he became. There was a sourness sprouting in his stomach. Something was wrong. Edward took care to control his breathing.

Both detectives continued to scan the horizon of spectators. It was a sea of black and white attire that melted everything together. Michael was exhausted from scouring the depths of the black-and-white abyss and needed a break. He placed his face into his hands, his elbows propped on his knees, and rubbed his eyes to clear them out.

Daniel was still locked in the crowd. Searching faces individually, still taking intermittent breaks to look at the crumpled photo from his pocket. Daniel's eyes scanned past another row when his mind told him to go back. Maybe it was instinct; perhaps it just took his mind a few seconds to register what his eyes had seen. There. A white male wearing an all-black tuxedo. Daniel could not pull his eyes away from the man's face. He forced his fixated eyes to look down at the picture and back up to the gentleman in all black. He exchanged a few more between the man and the photo; it was him.

As Daniel alternated his gaze between the man and the photo, he noticed the man was also distracted. With the rest of the crowd so intently honed into the music and the performers, this gentleman was making sporadic glances away from the focus of the venue's show into the gallery. Daniel remained fixated on him. He noticed that his glances were in the direction of Michael and him. With just a few more glances, Daniel knew he was looking at them.

"He's here," Daniel said softly, keeping a watch on their target. Michael's face shot up from his hands and into the crowd. A hot surge of adrenaline shot through his veins. "Where?"

"Sixth row from the bottom on the other side of the stage, maybe twenty or so seats in from the outer aisle. Don't stare, I think he sees us." Michael carefully counted the rows and seats until his eyes rested on him. He looked at the photo in Daniel's hand and looked back again. "Holy shit, that's him. You think he spotted us?"

"Yeah, I do."

"How so?"

"Well... for one, he keeps looking at us," Daniel replied matter-of-factly.

Daniel tried not to stare, but it was difficult. This was the man they had been hunting for months. Michael, too, was struggling not to stare through this man's soul. He nudged Daniel with his elbow. "Text the guys; let them know." Daniel pulled out his phone and inconspicuously texted Agent Duffey, *'He's here. Stay put. We'll let you know what we need.'* He slipped the phone back into his pocket.

Michael kept his watchful eye as the killer began to glance at them more frequently. The detectives avoided the dead giveaway for as long as possible, but plans never went accordingly. Michael looked back to find the killer was no longer glancing in their direction. He was staring right at them. Michael could feel his eyes lock with him. There was a moment where mentally he felt connected to him, that they both had acknowledged each other's presence, knowing exactly who each other was.

His heart rate began to rise. Detective Bradley had always seemed to manage his physiological response to stress well. Robberies, pursuits, and fights; he always remained calm and steadied breathing. This time was different. He could feel the anxiousness rise in him.

Their eyes remained locked. They were in a standoff across the gallery; each was waiting to see who would make the first move. After a few more seconds of the stare-down, the killer gave Michael a subtle head nod and then stood up. He casually slid down his row as the other guests sucked in their legs to allow room. The killer drifted into the outer aisle and disappeared behind a row of columns.

In the van outside the venue, Agent Duffey heard his phone vibrate on the metal shelf beside his laptop. He opened it and read the text. Feeling a rush of excitement hit his soul, he turned to Sergeant Lewis. "He's here. They've spotted him." Sergeant Lewis whirled around quickly, abandoning his sector of view through the windshield. "Seriously? What do they need from us?" Agent Duffey hesitated slightly, "Uh, nothing?"

"Huh?" Sergeant Lewis asked, confused and frustrated. Agent Duffey shrugged. "They just said to wait..."

"Those fuckers." Sergeant Lewis knew he could trust his detectives. Still, as a supervisor on scene, it was his duty to ensure this operation didn't go south. Sergeant Lewis liked to lead from the front, not the shadows. He was starting to get a nasty knot in his stomach.

The second the killer vanished from their eyesight, the detectives launched themselves out of their seats to the aisles, clipping the legs of every guest on their way. There were lots of grunts of contempt. The ruckus caught a few glances from the musicians below, still not missing a note between them.

Once they hit the aisle, they bolted up the stairs that separated the galleries and made their way to the lobby. As Michael approached the door, he tried to visualize in his head what direction he needed to go. Although right seemed the most logical decision, he knew the hallways formed a circle around the outside of the gallery, all connecting back to the lobby at the front. He was unsure if there were any fire exits along the way that the killer might utilize.

He reached the door to the outer hallway without missing a step, no doubt causing a stir again from the spectators. He stuck with his instincts and hooked right, barreling down the hallway with everything he had in him despite the restrictions of the tux. Daniel was trailing just behind him. Michael had started the chain reaction of running, and Daniel had no time to ask what the plan was. His trust was strong in Michael's instincts, and he followed suit. Daniel aggressively fought to get his phone from his pocket. He hoped to dial Sergeant Lewis, notify him, and simultaneously keep up with the killer. At the speed he was running, he could not break the phone from the tight tuxedo pocket; he abandoned the idea and focused on the chase.

Edward was running down the hall. He was out of breath almost instantly. Cardio had never been his strong suit. His adrenaline was the only fuel keeping him going. His feet radiated pain with every strike of the ground. His mind had gone into a panic. *'How the fuck did they find me? How do they know who I am?'* His thoughts raced madly, but there was no time to analyze them. All he needed to focus on now was getting away. He knew the men there were police. There was no other explanation for it. *'Were those the only two here?'* Edward had no plans on staying and finding out. He knew there could be others, and they would all be on high alert. Running down the hallway would only give him away. As he rounded the curved hallway, he saw a fire exit sign above him. He turned and hit the door with his body hard. The alarm screeched in a horrendous, high-pitched tone that was deafening.

Edward was on the sidewalk, still running. He knew his truck was only a few hundred yards from here, and he had no intention of stopping until he arrived. The cool air and heavy breathing from his mouth fueled a dry burn in his throat and lungs. He swallowed to lubricate it and maintained his stride.

The fire alarm howled throughout the halls. Detectives Bradly and Lugo halted, looking up at the red beacons on the walls, flashing a bright white strobe with every screech. Michael turned to Daniel, "Which way is it coming from?" Daniel looked around and threw his hands up, letting them clap back down against his hips. "I have no idea; I think one alarm triggers them all."

"FUCK! That means he's already outside. Call Sergeant, now! I'll head outside and see if he's still here." Daniel fumbled in his pocket once more and successfully retrieved his phone from his pocket. As he pulled it out to dial, a flood of spectators poured in from the gallery. No doubt, the ushers started flushing people out once the fire alarm rang.

"Jesus, fuck... call them now, dammit!" Michael barked as he turned and ran to the closest exit. He was not one to make orders to Daniel, but this was not a time he was willing to waste. Daniel pulled out his phone and saw Agent Duffey at the top of the 'recent calls' tab. He wouldn't waste time scrolling through his contacts for his Sergeant. He tapped Duffey's name and pulled the phone to his ear.

Sergeant Lewis and Special Agent Duffey sat anxiously in the van, waiting for any word from the detectives. Neither of them could sit still, knowing the killer was inside. Although Sergeant Lewis had the final say on how this operation would go, he was desperately telling himself he could trust the instincts of his detectives in their request for them to stay put in the vehicle.

"Do you hear that?" Agent Duffey turned to Sergeant Lewis with intense excitement. "Hear what?" Sergeant Lewis answered before his brain could even register the sound in question, but as the words left his lips, he heard it. "Fire alarm. It's gotta be him."

Agent Duffey felt his phone vibrating against his leg a few moments later. He reached in and pulled it out; it was Detective Lugo. Brad answered it and put it against his ear when something across the street in the parking lot caught his eye. His eyes were fixated on a white male in an all-black tuxedo. "That's him," Brad said, oddly calm, into the phone. "What?" Detective Lugo said in confusion but gave Brad no time to reply, "Hey! He's outside, he triggered the fire alarm, we're going to lose him!"

"I see him!" Brad said, still following him with his eyes. "Well, go after him!" Detective Lugo shouted into the phone. "Right," Brad replied, as his eyes shot to another moving object in his line of sight. This time, it was Detective Bradley running after the killer. He was struggling to close the distance. Michael was still crossing the opening of the sidewalk paths that led to the parking lot as the killer was entering the lot and disappearing into the maze of vehicles. "Gotta go," Brad said and quickly hung up the phone.

Detective Lugo looked down at his phone screen as the call disconnected. "What the fuck, man?" he asked out loud to no one. He threw his phone in his pocket and pushed through the crowd that had amassed in the halls. Agent Duffey turned to Sergeant Lewis, "Come on!" They both exited the vehicle and gave chase.

Edward could see his truck ahead. As he forced each leg to carry itself forward, the distance ceased to shrink in his mind. His adrenaline rush was dumping quickly. His gas gauge was far below 'E' but refused to quit. This was not how he would get caught; this was not how it would end. He still had work to do, and he intended to do it. He looked over his shoulder and made brief eye contact with the slightly out-of-shape cop in his cheap tux, doing his best to close the gap. As their eyes locked, the cop shouted something to him, but Edward paid no mind. Finally, he reached his truck. He grabbed the cold and rusty handle and snatched it open.

Detective Bradley was losing the race. The killer was bolting through the parking lot. Up ahead, in another lot adjacent to the theater's parking lot, was a black truck; he knew it was his. Michael mustered up the only breath he had left in him, "STOP, YOU MOTHERFUCKER!" The killer didn't stop. He was getting closer to the truck, and Michael could feel his legs and lungs failing him. He didn't anticipate many foot pursuits once he joined the Detective Bureau. The man had reached his truck and was climbing in as Michael hit his last stride; any further, his friends would be calling an ambulance for him. The truck revved loudly as it reared backward from its spot, through the parking lot, and onto the street. As it sped away, the license plate beamed to him. The first half of the plate, "Union, Charles, Yankee..." He said to himself. It was just as Benny had said. Michael could only get the following two numbers.

Michael heard a stampede of footsteps coming up behind him. He turned to see Daniel, Brad, and Sergeant Lewis all approaching him. "You let him get away?" Brad scoffed. His exhaustion turned to rage. "Are you fucking kidding me?" Michael asked, astonished at Agent Duffey's audacity. "Where the fuck is the van? Why didn't you stay in the van like we said? You could have kept up with him!" Agent Duffey looked to Sergeant Lewis, who averted his glance to the ground.

Michael looked to Daniel next, "Write down seven, six... It's the next two digits after what Benny provided to us." Daniel, who was lacking a pen and pad, pulled out his phone and wrote the digits down on a note. Michael continued, "The truck is a Ford, I saw red paint on the tailgate under the peeling paint; it's him." Daniel continued to type the information into his phone.

Agent Duffey chimed in, hoping Detective Bradley's anger towards him had dissipated: "I'll contact the State and give them a description. There are only a handful of routes he can take back to Emerald. There's a good chance a Trooper will pick him up."

"Yeah? Try a couple dozen routes, asshole," Michael fired at Agent Duffey; his anger had not receded. "You've been here a couple of weeks; you don't know shit. Daniel and I have been here our whole lives; there are dozens of backroad ways back home. If this asshole grew up here, too, then he probably knows them as well. He knows we're onto him now; he's not going to risk a main highway if he's smart, which apparently, he is… considering he just left us all with our dicks in our hands."

"Alright, Michael," Sergeant Lewis said, raising his hand and signaling him to cool it. "Michael's right. There are too many routes back home; there's no way he's staying on the main road. State probably has five or six troopers between here and Emerald. We will still give their dispatch a description for shits and giggles, but we can't rely on them to get him."

Sergeant Lewis was gathering his thoughts as the team rallied around him. Sergeant Lewis was no rookie and always had the voice of reason and logic. "Look, there's about five jurisdictions he can drive through depending on his route. We can't rely on state police to make a sighting and apprehension, and I won't have us wasting our time trying to call all the counties he might pass through. We know he's going back to Emerald. I know it. That's his safety net. Let's head back and start working with our own dispatch and records to see if we can link the partial plate to anything we've connected to in the past. Hopefully, in the two hours it takes us to return, we will have something to go off. This is not the end."

By now, everyone had seemed to catch their breath. Sergeant Lewis advised everyone to return to the vehicles they arrived in, mainly to separate Duffey and Bradley, giving everyone a chance to cool off. They all went back to their prospective cars and headed back west.

Chapter 34

Edward's heartbeat raced for nearly the first hour on the way back home before the pounding finally subsided. Once he got closer, calmness began to take over, and his nerves and breathing settled. Edward rolled his windows down and turned the radio off as he meditated on the engine's roar and the autumn air's soft breeze. He sensed his time may be coming to an end. Edward didn't know if his life would end with him in prison or in a coffin, but after the concert, he had a great fear one of those was coming. He knew there was a good chance that the police got his license plate. If not, perhaps a camera from the venue did that they would indeed seek out, or even his name from the seat reservation; the possibilities roamed wild in his head. He knew he had to be prepared.

His beaten truck pulled into the driveway. He swung into his usual spot of scarce gravel and dead grass and turned the engine off. He sat in the driver's seat briefly with the window still down. The cool breeze paired nicely with the sweat running down his face. He undid the tie of the tuxedo and opened the collar to let his skin breathe.

It was fully dark now. He could hear the shuffles and the mooing of the cows in the pasture beside his property, although it was too dark to see them. He looked up to the starlit sky, wondering how much longer he would enjoy this view. He turned his head back to the road; nothing but darkness. No red and blue lights flying down the road. No echo of a siren in the distance. *'Are they coming?'* He didn't know, but he knew tonight would be the night. If they didn't come by morning, there was a chance he would have made it away clean. But if they came, he would not be caught off guard.

Edward went inside and marched up the stairs quickly to his bedroom. He turned on the lamp on his nightstand, dimly lighting the room. Before heading up, he ensured no other lights in the house were on. He needed just enough light to see into the closet. He reached in and pulled out a rifle. It was an old military surplus M14 rifle. He had picked it up at a town pawnshop a few years back. Edward didn't know or care if the sale of old military weapons was legal, and he didn't think the shop owner cared either. All he knew was that he had wanted one since his adolescent years. It was such a beautiful rifle with so much history. The heavy wood stock felt nice in his hands. The owner had tried to sell Edward a scope and mount to put atop it; however, he declined. Edward liked the old iron sights. He felt it was more faithful to the gun.

He slid his hand up and down the smooth wood of the stock and held it up to his face, looking through the sites. It had been a while since he fired it; he didn't know if the sites were still zeroed. Edward never chose this rifle to make any of his kills. It was far too messy and too loud. But tonight, perhaps he would. He reached to the top shelf of the closet and pulled down a box of rounds. Only one box of twenty left. He knew if they came in numbers, it wouldn't last, but it may still make one hell of a standoff, and when he was down to just one round, he knew what he might have to do.

Edward loaded the rounds into the short magazine until it was complete. He then pulled the operating rod back and locked it open. He slid the magazine in until he felt it click into place and then released the operating rod to chamber a round. The clash of the metal was always exciting.

Now that the rifle was loaded, he walked over to the lamp and turned it off. Complete darkness encompassed him. He opened the drawer beneath the lamp and pulled out his small humidor of cigars. He selected one, cut and lit it, and then placed it into his mouth. Edward never smoked in the house, but it was a special occasion tonight. He perched himself up on a small stool next to the window that faced the road in front of his house and waited. He took a long drag from his cigar, rolling the smoke around in his mouth to get the deep flavor, and blew it out before him. He watched the smoke dance in the air before him until it drifted into darkness.

Chapter 35

It was well after dark when the detectives rolled back into Emerald. At Sergeant Lewis's direction, they took Route 360 West towards Emerald. At the same time, he and Special Agent Duffey traveled further south to Route 460 before heading west. Sergeant Lewis hoped that by splitting up, they would have some miraculous chance to cross the killer. However, they were not so lucky.

Detective Lugo stayed on the phone the entire drive back, trying to coordinate with dispatch and one of two records specialists who were far past the end of her shift per Sergeant Lewis's request. Daniel had Judy Andrews search their report system for any vehicle attached to a previous report containing a license plate with the alphanumerics obtained from the killer's plate. So far, the search has been turning up empty.

The detectives were only a few miles from the station when Daniel's phone beeped for an incoming call. He checked the screen and saw it was Sergeant Lewis. "Judy, I'm sorry I must cut you off. I'll call back soon."

"I'll be here," Judy replied, less than amused. Daniel answered the phone. "Hey, Sarge, we're almost back to the station."

"Don't. Stay mobile." He replied intently. "I think we might have a location."

"Seriously?" Daniel said, unable to contain his excitement. The tone of his voice intrigued Michael enough to take his eyes off the road momentarily. He mouthed *'What's up?'* to Daniel, but his request was brushed off.

"Whatcha got, Sergeant?" Daniel asked as he clicked his pen to prepare for any notes. "Well, I knew you were on the phone tied up with Judy. I went into Lenex on my phone to see if there was anything we could connect him to. I searched the partial license plate we got from his truck against all three zip codes that overlap Emerald. I left the make and model of the vehicle blank in the search tab in case the plates had been switched from another vehicle. I got a partial hit on three separate plates; one to a blue Honda Sedan, one to a black Dodge pickup, and one to a red Ford pickup." Sergeant Lewis paused for a minute before continuing when he got no answer from Detective Lugo. "Daniel, ask Michael if he's certain it was a Ford."

"Yes!" Michael shouted back over the phone from the driver's seat. He could hear from his position without Daniel having to repeat it. "You said the hit on the Ford was red, right?" He asked loudly so Sergeant Lewis could hear. "Red, that's correct."

"That's it!" Michael shouted as he triumphantly hit the steering wheel. "I know I saw red paint under the peeling black; it was a shitty cover paint job. Plus, it matches the chips found in the lab." Michael could barely contain himself in the seat.

"Then let's go with that. The plate shows it's registered to Edward Jackson, a white male. His residence is off Route 614, just a couple miles south of the school complex. I'll text you the address. Let's meet at the high school and wait for some road units to become available. I'll have Agent Duffey get back on the phone with State and have them send anyone available."

"We can't wait for that!" Michael shouted once again from the driver's seat. At this point, Daniel had placed the phone on speaker to reduce the need for his obscene speaking volume; however, Michael was far too antsy to control his tone or volume. "Sergeant," he continued, "We don't have time to wait. This guy knows he's been spotted. He may even assume we know who he is and where he's at. He could be packing his shit right now to leave and never come back. It might be too late if we wait for State or even a Tac team from a surrounding jurisdiction."

"So, what the hell are you proposing we do then, Michael?" Sergeant Lewis asked, almost agitated. Daniel held the phone in the empty space between Michael and himself, waiting for Michael to speak and break the silence. Let's go straight there and call in a few patrols to back us. Let's fucking end this thing."

Sergeant Lewis was not confident in this plan. His experience and better judgment told him to wait and play it smart. He, too, though, was worried Michael was right. Either play could pin medals on everyone's chest or risk a stack of reprimands. He looked over to Agent Duffy, who was driving the van. The look in his eyes showed he was with Michael, as well. Sergeant Lewis took a deep breath and let out a long, exhausted sigh. "How far out are you?" Michael instantly grinned as the words came through the phone. Daniel pulled the phone back to his face. "We're probably seven to eight minutes out."

"Okay," Sergeant Lewis acknowledged, looking at the GPS on his phone, "We're just a minute or two behind you. Don't fucking approach the house without me. Do you understand?"

"Of course," Daniel responded. "Michael?" Sergeant Lewis was explicitly worried about him. "Alright! Fine!" Sergeant Lewis took another breath and let another sigh follow its lead again. "Alright, I'll see you guys there. Be safe."

Chapter 36

Just a few minutes later, Detectives Lugo and Bradley were traveling down Route 614 when they first saw the house. "That's it," Detective Lugo said, not expecting a reply from Detective Bradley. He didn't get one. Michael looked to his right out the passenger side window past Daniel. It was a small, white, farmhouse-style home. It sat three to four hundred feet off the road. All the lights in the house were off, and the home was barely visible from the street. The only illumination of the home was from the bright moon and the stars scattered in the sky.

"Kill the lights," Daniel said to Michael. Michael reached up to the knob on the dash and rotated it. The lights went out, and only darkness was on the road in front of them. The road almost seemed to disappear, but Michael saw the remnants of the gravel driveway that led to the house and turned in, feeling the tires slide on the loose gravel for a split second before grabbing traction. He let his foot off the gas and let the car coast down the driveway towards the house. As the car settled to a stop, they stared up at the dark, seemingly empty house. Both were unaware of the occupant inside and that he was watching their every move.

"You wanna give it a walk around really quick before approaching?" Michael asked Daniel from the driver's seat. "Sergeant said to wait. Just a wide pan around, nothing up close," Michael answered to him. Daniel looked back up to the house into the dark windows, not seeing the eyes staring directly at him. Just then, Sergeant Lewis' and Agent Duffey's van could be heard coming down the quiet road. They both looked over their shoulders and saw the faint headlights a hundred yards down the road. "He's here anyway. Let's go," Daniel stated. They both got out of the car and began a slow walk to the house.

Daniel only made it a few steps when a loud crack rang out, resembling a large whip snapping in the air. Edward had sighted in on Daniel quickly and fired. The round ripped through Daniel's right shoulder, throwing him back against the hood of the car. "AAHHH!" Daniel screamed as he flopped onto the ground. Michael ducked to the ground with haste and crawled back behind the driver's side of the vehicle. Daniel was still exposed in front of the car.

Daniel began to drag himself back around the vehicle's passenger side towards the rear for cover, as the passenger side still left him exposed. "Daniel, are you okay?!?" Michael screamed from the other side of the vehicle. "He fucking shot me, man!" Daniel cried in pain. He continued to drag himself towards the rear of the car when a second shot rang out, striking Daniel once again in his left calf. "JESUS FUCK!" he howled. He kept his strength and finally made it behind the car. He let his face fall into the gravel-filled dirt and breathed through the pain that was almost too much to bear.

"Daniel, where the fuck are you?" Michael shouted again to him. "I'm behind the car. He fucking shot me, man, I'm bleeding everywhere!" He began to sob from the pain and spit a mouth of saliva as the words shot from his mouth, collecting in the dirt just a few inches from his face. "God dammit, man, it hurts so fucking bad." Michael could hear the pain and fear in his voice. Michael stayed low and crawled to the vehicle's rear to meet Daniel. "Everything's going to be okay, brother. I know it hurts, but it's nothing fatal, I don't think. You're going to make it, okay?" Michael said with as much assurance as he could. Daniel could only muster a pitiful and doubtful "Okay."

Sergeant Lewis and Agent Duffey were close enough to hear the second shot. They pulled in just after Michael had made it to Daniel. "Oh my god, I think he's hit," Brad said to Sergeant Lewis. Before the van even came to a halt, Brad jumped out and began to run to them. Michael saw Brad exiting the vehicle, hastily put his hand up, and shouted at him with everything in his lungs, "NO! STOP!" It was too late. Just a few feet away, the third shot was fired. Brad's body instantly went limp mid-stride and fell to the ground, smacking it like a two-hundred-pound rag doll. His body landed just two feet away from Michael and Daniel's position.

Michael reached out and grabbed Brad's limp arm and pulled his body towards him. Once close enough, he turned over his body to see how bad the damage was. As he rolled Brad towards himself, Michael recoiled at the sight. Half of Brad's face was gone, and a large hole on the right side of his head spilled brain matter from the opening. Michael let go and retreated from his body. He placed his face down onto Daniel's shoulder. "Don't look at him, he's dead."

"Fuck!" Daniel screamed in pain but also in fear that this would be the end of all of them.

Sergeant Lewis made it to their position safely. "How bad is he?" he asked Michael, unable to hide his concern. Brad's gone; Daniel's bad, but he'll make it." Sergeant Lewis looked over to Brad's body and then at Daniel. "You gonna make it, man?" Daniel looked up at him with tears strolling down his cheeks. "I can't move right now. I have to stay here."

Sergeant Lewis got on his phone and called the officer's line to dispatch. He advised them of shots fired and two men down. Dispatch called for all available units to respond and phoned the State Police dispatch requesting emergency response from any troopers in the area. Just a few moments later, they could hear the cavalry approaching from the distance. The sirens usually carried far, and the open country landscape made it cumbersome to estimate their arrival time.

Sergeant Lewis peeked up from the trunk of the car to the house. Another round cracked towards them, hitting the trunk lid; luckily, it did not penetrate the vehicle or the officers behind it. As the round exited the weapon towards Sergeant Lewis on the ground, a large muzzle flash escaped from the barrel. Sergeant Lewis had caught a glimpse of it as he ducked for cover, revealing the window it was coming from. *'I got you fucker.'* Sergeant Lewis took a deep breath and gathered his courage. He came back up from his cover while simultaneously punching his pistol out. The second his sights hit the window, he fired multiple shots and ducked back down. He waited to see if the killer would return fire, but he did not. The three of them held their position in silence. The killer had the high ground. With an entire house to move through and a wall full of windows to shoot through with no illumination, it was literally a shot in the dark for them.

Edward had his rifle positioned to fire from the open window when he saw the tall and muscular police officer come up from the vehicle. He dove to the floor, anticipating the incoming rounds; his reaction saved his life. As his body struck the old wood plank floor, the rounds entered sporadically through both the open bottom and the upper glass-shielded window. The bullets peppered his bedroom wall near the door. His position was no longer feasible to occupy. He gathered his rifle, got to his feet, and exited the room to head downstairs. He needed to change the battlefield and create distance. With his rifle against their pistols, it was no match. He had to get outside to win. Once downstairs, he ran out of the back door and through the yard. He hopped the fence separating his property from the neighbor's cow pasture and bolted for an ancient oak tree on the farm.

Michael had laid Daniel down in the dirt and let go to get up with Sergeant Lewis. They both peered over the vehicle's trunk to see into the house. No shots were fired towards them. "There's only one open window, the one he fired from. You think he's changing positions?" Sergeant Lewis asked Michael. "I don't know; at this point, he could be anywhere in there. We need to wait for backing units before we try approaching and can set up a perimeter."

At this point, the sirens were less than a few hundred yards away. They would be there within the minute. Another noise caught his attention as Michael scanned the house against the sirens. The mooing of a group of cows from just behind the house on the adjacent property. Michael's eyes naturally wandered to the field. There, in the moonlight, he saw the killer's figure running. He was at full sprint with a long rifle in his hand. At this point, there was no waiting for those sirens to arrive. This was their chance.

"He's running!" Michael shouted to Sergeant Lewis and bolted from behind the car. He gave no chance of acknowledgment. It took Sergeant Lewis a moment for his brain to register what Michael had said, and then he took off after him.

As Michael neared the fence, he threw his weapon into his holster to avoid a negligent discharge. He cleared the fence and immediately drew it back out. Sergeant Lewis followed just a few steps behind.

Edward looked back as he traversed the field. He saw the two officers that were trailing him. There was still a fair amount of distance, and stopping to take a shot would allow them to advance, but a landed shot would be worth the risk. He stopped dead in his tracks, turned, and aimed the rifle at the officers. Just as he began to squeeze the trigger, both officers dove in opposite directions of each other, landing in the high pasture grass and concealing their position. The shot split the air between them and continued into the darkness.

Edward lowered the weapon from his sight and turned to run again. He had just crested the hill towards the oak tree when three shots rang out in quick progression behind him. After Edward's shot, Michael had gained his composure quickly and came to a kneeling position. He brought his weapon back to his line of sight and settled on the killer running away a great distance ahead of him. Michael pulled the trigger three times as quickly as his finger allowed for. Two rounds struck Edward.

Edward screamed out in pain. One round entered his lower left buttocks and exited through his lower left hip. The other ripped through his left thigh. His rifle fell from his hands as he grabbed the back of his thigh, still grunting through the shock of the pain. He stumbled a step further before his legs could no longer carry him. He fell to the ground, clutching the wounds with his hands and cursing through the pain.

Michael watched the man drop into the high grass and disappear. He had seen the weapon fall from his hands, but it was unclear if he could regain possession of it once on the ground. He looked over to Sergeant Lewis, who was still gathering himself and getting up to his knees to see. "Are you okay?" Michael whispered to him. "Yeah, I'm fine. Did you hit him?"
"Yeah, I think I did," Michael answered as he looked back towards the killer, awaiting a possible resurgence from the grass, but none came.

"I'm not sure where he's hit. Flank him to the right, and I'll take the left; just stay out of my path of fire." Michael motioned to Sergeant Lewis with his firearm as he spoke. Sergeant Lewis took to his feet and began to approach the killer from the far-right side as Michael did to the left.

The two approached him slowly until he came into view. Michael had his weapon on the killer steadily as he stepped up to him, spotting his rifle just a few feet away. Although out in the dark, the moonlight lit up the killer's blood that had leaked from his lower body into the flattened grass around him. "Don't you fucking move, asshole," Michael said, looking straight into the killer's pained eyes. The killer said nothing, but his soulless eyes broke from his gaze and drifted up to the sky. He was still grunting in pain and holding his leg and hip.

Sergeant Lewis removed a set of handcuffs from his belt and approached him. He pulled the killer's arms from where he was holding his wounds and rolled him over, bringing his hands behind his back. The killer let out a low scream in pain that only added to the satisfaction of Sergeant Lewis and Michael.

Emerald Police patrol officers were now arriving on the property. Michael looked over and saw the first one exiting his patrol car, running to Daniel and giving aid. A second one joined soon after, and a third ran past to Michael and Sergeant Lewis' position.

Michael looked down at the killer. They locked their eyes and stared into each other, neither saying a word. Michael broke from the stare and looked over to Sergeant Lewis. Michael had become overwhelmed with grief and relief at this moment; tears began to stroll down his cheeks. Sergeant Lewis gave him a head nod and simply said, "Good job. I'll send a patrol back here to help you gather him up. Are you good with him?" Michael, who now had a waterfall down the front of his face, nodded modestly. Sergeant Lewis bent over and grabbed the rifle from the ground. He cleared it, sticking the magazine and the round from the chamber into his pockets, and wandered off to the vehicles.

Minutes later, an ambulance arrived on the scene. Daniel was patched up by paramedics and loaded onto a stretcher just as Edward was being dragged up to a patrol car and stuffed into the back seat. As the paramedics loaded Daniel into the bus, he got his first close-up look at the killer.

"How are you holding up?" Michael's voice entered his mind. The question broke Daniel's focus on the killer. He looked over to his disheveled partner. "I'll make it. That's him, huh?" Daniel already knew the answer to his question, but for his own sanity, he needed to hear that all this madness was over. "It is. But you don't need to worry about him right now. Get to the hospital; I'll call your wife for you. I'm sure Sargeant will send a unit to drive her to you at the hospital."

"Okay," Daniel said in a defeated voice. His mixed emotions remarkably matched those of Michael's. He watched the patrol officer pull off the property with the monster in the back, no doubt taking him to the same hospital he would be at soon. Daniel finished his conversation with Michael, and the paramedics closed the door to the bus and pulled off. As the ambulance traveled down the road, Daniel looked out the rear window to the house, watching it disappear into the darkness just as it had emerged to them from it just a short while earlier. Daniel closed his eyes and rested his head back on the stretcher. Although in immense pain, his body allowed him to drift off into a light state of sedation. His mind cleared, and sleep brought the darkness he needed.

Chapter 37

"Hey buddy, how are you feeling?" Daniel woke up from a light sleep in a hospital bed to Michael's words. As he tried to sit up, it became pretty evident that the pain meds were wearing off. A sharp pain shot through his shoulder as he slid up on the elevated mattress. He looked up to his friend Michael, who seemed genuinely concerned about his well-being. "I'm alright, I guess. I'm alive. After everything, I at least have to be grateful for that." They both exchanged a silent gaze with each other.

"What about Brad? Has his family been notified?" Daniel asked, trying to hold back a choked voice sneaking in. "Sergeant Lewis called the Richmond field office and asked if he could notify the family himself since he was there with him. He got ahold of his sister and said she would tell their mother herself. It's gonna be a few weeks before they hold a funeral for him; full honors, of course." Daniel just nodded to Michael as he finished speaking, thinking of what to say next.

"What about that asshole? Where's he at?" Daniel asked with a touch of anger. Michael looked up to the ceiling. "Oh, he's two floors above you. Each hand is cuffed to a rail, two uniforms on him at all times, you know the game." Daniel answered with a nod again. "So? He's really it, huh? I'm assuming you've already questioned him? Assuming he can speak, that is."

"Oh yeah. He's fine; he took two rounds to the lower half. He admitted to everything." Daniel looked up, astonished. "Really? How much convincing did that take?"

"None, really," Michael said as he shrugged his shoulders. "It was almost as if he was anxious to tell his story. I never understand it; try so hard to get away, and then squeal like a stuck pig the second you get caught. But hey, commend yourself. You were right about the music pieces." Daniel's head leaned back. "Damn, what was the significance of it?" he asked bewildered. "Nothing, honestly. The fucker just liked the music, I guess. Spewed some shit about 'it's so beautiful it makes you sad.' However, he was able to recount all the murders and provide details that were never released to the media. It's him. Sergeant Lewis and I already executed a warrant on his truck and home; found traces of blood from Shannon Reed in the back room of his home, found hairs from a few girls in his truck."

Daniel sighed deeply as he laid his head back down and looked up to the ceiling. "It's over then, huh? All those months of work, finally over."

"Well," Michael said unenthusiastically, "we still have the trial and the circus that comes along with that. But we have his confession on recording, so it should be fine. Who knows how many months it will be before that gets set."

"Yeah," Daniel replied with a raised eyebrow. Anyway, what's his status? Is he going to be here awhile?"

"Nah," Michael replied. He had surgery two days ago, the same as you. He's got another week or so of recovery before he can be moved. I'll be sure to be gentle with him." They both shared a chuckle.

"Look, man," Michael said, interrupting the silence. Get some rest. I'll come check on you again tomorrow." "Make sure you check to see if my wife is here first. She might kick your ass for letting me get shot." Daniel laughed and then cringed from an onset of pain. "Tell her once you're better, I'll give you some dodgeball lessons, so it doesn't happen again." Both detectives laughed again. "I love you, brother; thanks for getting me out of there alive." Michael looked to the dull tile floor, fighting back tears in his eyes. "I love you too, man. And of course. I just didn't want to deal with training a new partner." They both had tears in their eyes now and smiled to fight them back. Michael leaned down and gave Daniel a hug. They exchanged their goodbyes, and Michael left the room.

Chapter 38

One day after Michael visited Daniel, Edward awoke in the same hospital. As his eyes opened, he felt a surge of pain shoot down from his left hip down through the entire leg. The doctors were obviously being stingy with the pain meds. *'They don't give a fuck about me.'*

As Edward continued to shuffle, a uniformed officer stepped into the room. "You awake, Mr. Jackson?" Edward looked up, honestly shocked that the officer used his manners in talking with him. "Yeah, I guess." Edward attempted to shrug but only had half the normal range of motion from the handcuffs connecting him to the rails on either side of the bed. The officer spoke again. "You've got a visitor, been waiting out in the lobby for damn near two days now."

Edward attempted to rub his eyes when he heard the snag of the chained cuffs. *'Duh, dumbass.'* Edward gathered his thoughts momentarily and looked back up to the officer. "Who the hell is here to visit me?" Edward said in a genuinely curious tone. "Detective Bradley said she was claiming to be your sister," The officer answered him. Confusedly, Edward replied, "Who the hell is Detective

Bradley?" The officer just raised an eyebrow and shook his head as he turned around to exit the room. Edward looked down at his bandaged-wrapped leg. *'Oh, right.'* The officer spoke as he left the room. "The detective said she could visit with you for a few minutes; I'll grab and escort her back to you."

Edward was suddenly nervous. It had been a while since he had spoken to his sister. He didn't know what to expect from her. Was she angry? Sad? Just happy to see him? Her reaction could be anything when she walked in.

Only a few moments later, he could hear footsteps shuffling down the hall's tile floor. Edward's heart began to race. A second later, she rounded the corner with the uniformed officer in tow. He told her he would be outside the door and cracked it to give them privacy.

She struggled to look up from the floor as she wandered into the corner and sat in the black pleather chair. It was apparent she had been crying for days. There was a hurt in her eyes that Edward had not seen since the death of their mother. She sat still for a moment, gathering her composure.

"Elaine... I wasn't..."
"You're all over the news right now. That's how I found out about all of this. We've barely spoken over the years. These killings... all those girls. I had followed it all on the news the past few months but never imagined..." She trailed off as she began to sob. Edward didn't get emotional often but never liked seeing his baby sister cry. Even if his baby sister was an adult now.

"Elaine, I'm sure this is a lot to take in right now. I'm sure you have so many questions. I'm unsure if I can answer all of them, but I'd like to help you deal with this if possible." There was dead silence for a few moments before Edward continued. "I never thought I was a monster like those people on television are saying. I knew there was something inside of me, but..." Elaine cut him off.

"Edward, I just have one question. And I need you to be honest with me. That's all I need from you. After all these years of struggling, I need you to tell me the truth. You can even take a few minutes to think about lying to me, but when you're done, I need to know the truth." Edward just blankly stared back at her. He wasn't exactly sure what she was about to ask, but in his heart, he told himself that he would do his best to be honest with her.

She looked up at him, with tears still rolling down her bright, rosy cheeks. Her voice was shaking as she spoke. "Did you do it?" She gritted the words out of her mouth as if it pained her to ask. Edward stared back at her. He didn't want to lie to her, but he didn't want to cause her any more pain. He took a deep breath and sighed as it exhaled back out of him.

"It's true. Everything you've seen on the news, read in the papers. It's all true. I never meant to become this man..."

"Not that, Edward." She interrupted sternly, almost angry. She seemed to grit her teeth as she continued to speak. "I'm not talking about those girls on the television, Edward. I already know about all of that. I've already spoken to the detectives. I know it was you that did that. That's not what I'm asking you."

Edward now knew precisely what she meant. This was not the question he was prepared for, but deep down, he always knew it was coming. His eyes shifted to the floor briefly before she re-engaged him.

"Edward. Was it you? Did you do it?" He continued to stare at her, speechless, almost emotionless. He didn't have the words inside him to speak, but she didn't give up. "Just tell me the truth, Edward. Tell me it was you. I know it was you. I've always known it was you." His eyes locked with hers in a dark battle for dominance. *'Have you always known? If you've always known, why haven't you said anything? You didn't know.'*

"I need you to tell me it was you, Edward. I know it was you!" Her tone was straight anger now. Saliva spit from her mouth as she spoke. Her face was red, and tears were now unstoppable, cascading from her eyes. "Was it you, Edward?"

"Was it you..."

"Was it you..."

Chapter 39

Twelve months had passed since the incident at the farmhouse on Route 614. It had been a long and mundane year for Edward. It was nearly six months after his arrest before the trial occurred. The trial was a two-week monotonous affair. Edward's lawyer didn't have much of a defense after he confessed to the murders. His attorney's only course of action was pleading not guilty by reason of insanity. While most people would argue that Edward was insane, the court-appointed psychologist and the court did not agree. He was subsequently found sane and convicted of first-degree murder on all counts.

One full day of the trial only consisted of family impact statements. Multiple members from each family came up to the podium. One by one, they told their story of what they had lost and could never get back. They told stories of a future without the lost ones and how they would never recover from the trauma inflicted upon them by

Edward Jackson. The emotions waved back and forth between sadness, anguish, and anger.

At the end of the family impact statements, Edward was afforded an opportunity to speak to the court and families. He declined to make a statement. Edward knew nothing he would say would change anything. It would not give the families more closure, it would not bring the dead ones back, and it would not bring forgiveness for him. Mostly, however, he didn't speak because he didn't care. He didn't care about forgiveness. He didn't care about their closure. He didn't care about showing remorse because he didn't have any. He played his game for a while and eventually lost. Here he was to start a new, isolated life. Edward was given life in prison without the chance of parole.

Edward was sent to Sussex State Prison. His time in prison had not been easy. He was attacked and beaten several times in just the first few weeks of his stay. Many inmates who had not seen their wives, daughters, and girlfriends in years took quite an issue with a man who slaughtered them so emotionlessly and so heinously. The last beating had put him in the infirmary for nearly two weeks. Edward was jumped in the shower and stabbed in his left abdomen.

Although the guards and Warden felt no sympathy for Edward, their responsibility was to keep him safe. After a few discussions, Edward was placed in protective isolation, alone in a cell and with little exposure to other inmates. It was a change that Edward welcomed greatly. Once in isolation, he was able to rest, rest that he had needed for many years.

Edward's time in prison also brought the challenge of dealing with his urges. Chronic masturbation was the only remedy that kept him from going insane from the lack of opportunity he had to kill and violate other women.

Edward knew in his mind that he would never survive here. If not for other inmates taking his life, he only assumed that he would eventually take his own. The nothingness was already killing him inside. His mind was dying more each day, and before long, he would be nothing more than the shell of a man, a hollow body with no purpose and no hope. Edward spoke to himself every day, *'You just keep going until you can't go anymore.'* It was a promise to himself that he would end it when he could bear it no more.

'You just keep going until you can't go anymore.'

Epilogue

"Jackson, you have a visitor." Correctional Officer Heisman said as he walked up to Edward's cell door. Edward looked up to the prominent officer, confused, "I thought I wasn't allowed to have any visitors?" The guard chuckled. "This one got special approval from the Warden, some sort of doctor. I'm sure he's gonna write some sort of book or something that glorifies you." The guard chuckled again annoyingly. "Anyway, since you're in protection, we're gonna set up a chair for him to speak to you here. Be back in a few minutes." The guard returned a few minutes later and slammed down a chair in front of the cell.

Moments later, he could hear the shuffling footsteps of two individuals. One was presumably the guard escorting, and the other was his visitor. Edward didn't know who would care to come see him. "Here you are," Edward heard Heisman say to the visitor, still unseen. "Warden told me to give you guys some privacy."

"Why thank you, Officer, much appreciated," The visitor answered. Edward's ears and interest peaked. His voice was so familiar yet couldn't be placed in his mind.

The visitor's feet shuffled a few feet further until he was in view. The clothing style and face immediately triggered a memory in Edward's mind, Doctor Harold Kramer. The man who assisted Doctor Brown at his therapy session, a session that Edward had long ago forced himself to forget.

"Hello, Edward. It's been quite some time; I hope you are doing well." Doctor Kramer looked around Edward's cell briefly before continuing, "Well, doing well, considering the circumstances. Tell me, Edward, how have you been?"

"I've been better," Edward replied, unenthused. Doctor Kramer laughed lowly, "Yes, indeed, you probably have. I'm sure you're wondering why I'm here." Edward looked him up and down before answering. "I sure hope it's not to give me another therapy session. The last one didn't go so great."

"Oh, really?" Doctor Kramer asked in an amused tone. I thought it went quite well. I felt so close to unlocking a part of your mind that perhaps you had long forgotten- one that you may have thought never existed." Edward annoyingly rolled his eyes and sat straight on his bed, forcing himself to make eye contact with the strange doctor. "Oh yeah? What part would that be?"

"Oh, we can get to that in just a second." Doctor Kramer answered.

"Look, if you're here to write an article or a book or something, I don't know if I can tell you anything the cops haven't already told to the media. Maybe some finer details of the killings, but maybe if someone donated a few dollars to my commissary, I'd remember a bit more. Food in the kitchen here is kinda shit."

Doctor Kramer cleared his throat and pulled out a small grey notebook. It appeared to be a pleasant and smooth suede material with some gold imprint on the cover; Edward couldn't tell exactly what it was. "Well, Edward," Doctor Kramer said and paused, "I would like to write something on you for sure, with your permission, that is. But of course, I need something that no one else has if I plan to sell anything. And, of course, if it sells, I wouldn't mind affording you some commodities for a slightly more comfortable life."

"So, what would you like to know about?" Edward asked, slightly more intrigued.

"Well, first, Edward. Have you spoken to your sister? I found her number. I attempted to speak with her. I had a few questions that I thought she might be able to answer for me. She had no interest in speaking with me, but it was quite apparent that she knew the answer to what I was looking for. So, tell me, have you spoken to her? Does she know?"

"Know what?"

"Oh, I think you know, Edward. I was so close to revealing it in our session. That is until our friend, Doctor Brown, stopped it. But I think we both know what you saw in that vision, Edward. And I need you to say it. I need you to tell me all about it."

Edward was fixated on him now. Their eyes locked together, unable to look away. Edward already knew what he was going to ask. What his sister was asking over a year ago in the hospital. Edward never answered her question. Elaine stormed out of the hospital room; he hadn't heard from her since. Doctor Kramer spoke again. Their eyes still locked in a dark trap "So, Edward. I want to know. Tell me about the night you killed your mother…"

The End.

A Forward To My Next Work

"Whether he is your brother in flesh or your brother in arms, to betray him is a sin. And although God may not punish you on this physical earth for your actions, the Devil will fuel those betrayed to seek revenge. Be warned; the Devil is right behind you."

- J.E. Street III